SYCAMORE LANE

Stacey Horan

ISBN: 1503335127

ISBN 13: 9781503335127

Library of Congress Control Number: 2014921070

CreateSpace Independent Publishing Platform

North Charleston, South Carolina

ACKNOWLEDGMENTS

Thank you to Scott Collard for his enthusiasm and valued contributions, and to Beth Terrill for her professional advice and editing. Thank you to my family for being such ardent cheerleaders. Most of all, thank you to Matt, my wonderful husband and best friend, for his unfaltering support and for reading this book so many times he can probably recite it by heart.

To Matt, with all my love.

SATURDAY, SEPTEMBER 3ᴿᴰ

"**H**appy Moving Day, Everyone!" I read aloud. I roll my eyes. The message is scrawled in giant yellow letters across the blackboard paint covering one wall of the bedroom. "Well, it is moving day, but I wouldn't exactly call it happy." I continue talking even though no one can hear me. "Nine moves in fourteen years. I'm an expert on moving days, and none of them has been particularly fun. I don't expect this one to be any different."

I walk around the room while talking to myself, inspecting the closet and the view from the windows. My parents just bought this house, and today is the first day I'm seeing it. This has been a really quick move, even for semi-professional relocators like us. We're in New York this time, but it doesn't really matter. Just when I get used to this place, we'll pick up and move again. I hear my mother's advice from this morning in my head, "Sweetheart, moving is an opportunity. You can either stand up and make yourself known, or you can hide. The choice is yours." I roll my eyes again. It's the same advice she gives me every time we move.

Frankly, the only choice I'm concerning myself with at the moment is picking which of the two bedrooms I want, but that's a pretty easy decision to make. I'm going to take the other bedroom. This one is much too small, and it's painted *Superman* blue of all colors. It actually hurts my eyes to look at it. Besides, it has this stupid, childish blackboard wall. Surely Mom and Dad will paint over it. I'm a little too old for stuff like that. I'm fourteen, or "fourteen going on twenty-four" as Dad says a lot. I stand in the middle of the room, hands on my hips, and announce, "I'm definitely not taking this room."

As I say this, the ceiling light turns off. It flickers on and off a few times and then turns off again. "Fantastic!" I say as I throw up my hands. "Bad wiring. Can't wait to see what else is wrong with this place." I reach for the light switch on the wall and flip it. The ceiling light turns on. I toggle the switch up and down, and the light turns on and off as it should. "Weird," I say. "One more reason not to take this room."

I hear the front door open. That must be Dad. I race down the stairs and find my parents sitting on the front porch steps. It's the closest thing to a sofa or chairs that we've got at the moment, so I join them. Dad found a bagel shop, and he passes out bagels wrapped in wax paper. He hands Mom an extra large cup of coffee and me a pint of orange juice. I open the wax paper and take a bite of the bagel.

"Eat up. We're going to need the energy," says Dad with a giddy smile. Clearly, he is very excited about this move. I only wish I shared his enthusiasm. A couple of weeks ago Dad mentioned that his company was transferring him (yet again), and now here we are at 19 Sycamore Lane in a two-story grey house with white trim and black shutters.

After a few minutes, Dad asks, "So, how is it?"

"*Mmmm hmmm*," I say with a mouth full of food. The bagel is surprisingly good.

"I'm glad it meets with your approval, Lulu," says Dad as he takes the lid off his cup of coffee to let it cool.

My parents insist on calling me Lulu. It's been their pet name for me since I was a baby. Secretly, I kind of like it, although I beg them not to call me Lulu in public. They're pretty good about remembering, but there's always a risk that they'll slip up. I tend to get teased if other kids find out. In first grade, Mom called me Lulu when she came to help in my classroom one day. From that day onward all the kids called me "*Doo-doo.*" Fortunately, we moved at the end of that year. My name is actually Tallulah. I was named after an old movie actress, Tallulah Bankhead. Mom says she was colorful, vivacious and uninhibited. I'm none of those things, so the name is wasted on me.

We finish our bagels as the moving truck pulls up to the curb.

"Perfect timing," says Mom. She gathers the wax paper and napkins and heads inside.

"All right, kiddo," says Dad as he claps his hands together. "Let's get this house in order, shall we?" I nod and smile.

* * *

By noon, most of my stuff has been deposited in my new bedroom. It's even bigger than my last bedroom, which so far is the only positive thing to come out of this move. Mom said the prior owners had twin daughters who shared this room. It would be a tight fit for two people, but there's plenty of space for me. The prior owners also had a little boy, hence the other room painted *Superman* blue with a blackboard wall.

I'm in the middle of folding clothes and putting them in my dresser when Dad pokes his head through the doorway. "Hey, Lulu. Your mom wants me to walk into town and pick up some sandwiches for lunch. Want to come with me?"

"Sure!" I answer. "I'll be right down."

I head to the bathroom to splash some water on my face and run a brush through my hair. When I finish, I pass by the blue room and something catches my eye. At this point, the room contains only a spare chair, a couple of lamps and some boxes marked 'Miscellaneous.' But what catches my attention is the blackboard wall, which is opposite the door.

"What the...?" I mumble as I stand in the doorway.

Much of the writing on the wall has been erased, but a few chalk letters remain: the 'H' from Happy, the 'i' from Moving, the 'D' from Day, the 'E' from everyone, and the '!'. The surviving letters are spread out across the length of the wall, but they actually form a word.

"H i D E !," I read aloud. "So weird."

I run down the stairs taking the last two in one jump and say, "Hey, did either of you guys wipe off the blackboard upstairs?"

"What blackboard?" says Dad, grabbing his wallet for our trip into town.

"The one in the blue room. You know, it has one wall painted to be a blackboard. Someone had written 'Happy Moving Day, Everyone' in yellow chalk."

"Happy Moving Day, huh?" repeats Dad.

"Yes, that's what it said," I reply. "Most of it was erased. Now it just says, 'Hide'."

"Hide?" asks Mom. "Sorry, darling. It wasn't me. Perhaps one of the movers did it."

"Don't know anything about it, kitten," says Dad. "Are you ready to go?" I nod my head, and he holds the front door open for me.

It only takes fifteen minutes for us to walk to town, and it's a nice stroll through a neighborhood with very fancy houses. No complaints there. The town is quaint but lively, and we find a busy deli located between a pizzeria and an ice cream shop. I'm starting to love this town.

We take the sandwiches to go and head for home. On the way back, Dad offers a suggestion, "Let's take a little detour, Lulu, so we can get a look at your new school. What do you say?"

"Fabulous," I answer with very little enthusiasm. I don't really want to get a look at the school. I'd rather postpone that for as long as possible. Ninth grade starts in three days, and I'm not looking forward to it.

As we approach the school grounds, my stomach starts doing somersaults. The school itself is beautiful – three stories of red brick and white stone with lots and lots of windows. There is a huge banner hanging from the roof. It reads, "Welcome Back Mongooses!"

"Seriously?" I ask. "The mascot is a mongoose?"

"Apparently," answers Dad. "Don't underestimate the mongoose, Lulu. It might not be very big, but it's quite scrappy. I certainly wouldn't mess with it." He puts his arm around my shoulder and gives me a squeeze. "It's a tough little thing, just like you."

I roll my eyes and reply, "Hardly." I've never, ever been accused of being tough. In fact, it's probably the last word I would use to describe myself.

"And," he says, giving me another squeeze. "The real estate agent told us there are only about 1,000 students in the whole school. You'll get lots of individualized attention. Isn't that great?"

I fake a smile. That's definitely not what I want to hear. I like to blend in, hide in a crowd. I'm pretty shy generally, although I am working on being more outgoing. I do the math in my head.... 1,000 kids in a school that goes from kindergarten through twelfth grade. My stomach does another flip. I think of the remaining chalk letters on the blackboard wall. "Fat chance," I whisper under my breath. How do you hide when there are only 75 students in the entire ninth grade?

SUNDAY, SEPTEMBER 4ᵀᴴ

When I wake up in the morning, it takes me a few moments to realize where I am. I rub my eyes and crawl out of bed, still wearing my clothes from moving day. I stand in the hallway and stretch. A few muscles are actually sore from yesterday, muscles I didn't even know I had. I notice that my parents' bedroom door is open. They must be downstairs already. I peak into their room and find boxes everywhere.

"It's going to take them forever to get this place cleaned up," I mutter to myself. I shake my head and back out of the room. I stick my head in the blue room to survey the damage before heading downstairs. Boxes and furniture are piled high in the middle of the room leaving about a two-foot wide path between the walls and all the stuff. Basically, everything that didn't have an obvious place somewhere else in the house has ended up in here. I glance at the blackboard wall. The remaining letters, "H…i…D…E…!," have been erased. I swear they were still on the blackboard when I went to bed last night. "Odd," I mumble and head downstairs.

I find my way to the kitchen. Clearly my parents haven't unpacked their coffee maker yet, because Dad has made another run to the bagel shop. There's an unwrapped bagel and a pint of orange juice sitting on the table for me in front of any empty chair, and both my parents are sipping hot coffee from extra large to-go cups.

"Good morning, sweetheart," says Mom as she looks up from her newspaper. "Did you sleep well?"

"Yeah, great," I reply. "I must have passed out last night. I don't remember a thing. Is this for me?"

"Sure is," answers Dad without looking up from his newspaper.

"I'm afraid so," says Mom. "I'll go to the grocery store later today, but it's bagels again this morning."

"Fine with me," I say as I use my finger to scrape the extra cream cheese from the wax paper and smear it on the bagel. "Hey, did either of you guys wipe off the blackboard upstairs?"

"What, kitten?" asks Dad as he turns a page of his newspaper.

"The blackboard upstairs," I repeat. "Did you erase the last few letters?"

"Not me, Lulu" answers Dad, again without looking up.

"There are quite a few boxes in that room," says Mom. "Maybe the movers brushed up against it and erased it. If you'd like, I can pick up some chalk today when I'm at the store."

"Sure," I say before remembering that I thought the blackboard wall was stupid and childish. "I mean, if you want to. We should probably have some chalk in the house in case any of the neighbor kids come over and want to draw."

"Of course," says Mom with a smile. "In case the neighbor children would like to draw. That would be nice." She goes back to reading her newspaper, still smiling. I hate it when she sees right through me. She's spooky that way.

I finish my bagel and most of my orange juice before speaking again. I've been thinking about the movers, and it just doesn't make any sense. "I don't think the movers did it."

"Did what?" asks Dad as he turns another page.

I sigh loudly. Has he not been paying attention? "Erase the blackboard upstairs. I don't think they did it. I mean, they might have rubbed part of it off yesterday, but there was still some writing on the board last night. Obviously they didn't rub it off *after* they left. No, I don't think it was them...or at least not *just* them. So who could have done it?"

"I agree," says Dad as he continues to read. "Sounds like a plan. You should do that." Clearly he's not paying any attention.

Mom chimes in before I can respond. "I wouldn't worry about it, sweetheart. I'll pick up some chalk, and you can write whatever you want on the wall. Won't that be nice?" She sips her coffee and picks up another section of the newspaper.

I look back and forth at both of them. They don't appear to find this curious at all. I watch them for a few minutes. They just sip, read, sip, read. I crumple my empty wax paper and give up.

* * *

From my bedroom window, I see Mom's car pull into the driveway. She's back from the grocery store. I should go down and help her, but I'm still practicing. Mom, of all people, would understand. There's no sense in stopping mid-movement. I'm working on Poulenc's Sonata for Piano and Flute. I have the piano part down. That was fairly easy to learn, but now I have to learn the flute part. That's the rule in this house. If you're going to play it, play all of it. I like the flute. It's one of my better instruments, but it's not my favorite. My real love is the piano, but ours hasn't been delivered yet. So, if I want to get any practicing done, it's flute, clarinet, trumpet or violin. And I'll take the flute over the others any day. I find it to be the easiest. I'm proficient at the clarinet and trumpet, but I don't feel passionate about them. I do feel passionate about the violin, but I still stink at it. If I practiced more, I'd get better, but it's just more fun to play something I'm naturally good at.

As soon as I finish playing the last note I hear Mom call my name. She's not going to let me get away with playing something else until I've helped her in the kitchen. I put my flute on the music stand and head downstairs. I enter the kitchen as Mom places the last grocery bag on the kitchen counter. I start on the bags containing milk and other refrigerated items because that stuff is the easiest to unpack. Mom starts organizing the pantry. Once the cold items are put away, I rummage through the remaining bags and discover a box of chalk at the bottom of the bag containing laundry detergent and toilet bowl cleaner.

"White? They didn't have any colored chalk?" I whine.

"Sorry, darling. That's all they had," replies Mom. "And you're welcome."

"Thanks, Mom," I mumble. I grab the chalk and head for the stairs.

"Finish helping me put these groceries away, please, before you go running off," calls Mom. I return to the kitchen, sigh heavily, and finish emptying grocery bags. Putting everything away takes twice as long as normal because Mom keeps changing her mind as to where she wants me to put stuff. I finally can't take it anymore. I grab the last couple of items, shove them in the pantry and close the door.

"All done," I announce. "Can I go now?"

"Yes, Lulu. Thanks for helping me," says Mom as she opens the pantry door to start rearranging everything. "Don't go too far, though. The piano is being delivered this afternoon, so I'm going to need your help later in the conservatory. We need to clear out some boxes so the delivery guys can get in there."

Mom is a musician, too. That's where I get my love of music. However, she is infinitely more talented than I am. She can play any instrument known to man. Sometimes I get so jealous of her. She's taught me everything I know, but I have a long way to go before I'm anywhere near as good as she is. She even started giving me pipe organ lessons last year. Now, that's a pretty cool instrument. I'm hoping we can find an organ somewhere around here so I can continue to learn how to play. Mom has played in orchestras everywhere we've lived, and she's played whatever instrument they've asked her to play. It's sickening, really.

At our last house she started giving music lessons in our living room and really enjoyed it. Fortunately, this new house has an extra room in the back, right off the living room. It is plenty big enough to fit the piano and her music stands, and it has a lovely bay window that looks out onto the backyard where some of the rose bushes still have blooms on them. She's so excited to have her own music room. Mom says it's the main reason she and Dad decided to buy this house.

"I'll be upstairs," I say as I leave the kitchen, hoping that she'll forget that she's asked me to help her later. I decide that flute practice can wait. There's no sense in reminding her that I'm in the house and available for manual labor. I think something quiet and inconspicuous is in order. I stop by my room and rummage through my dresser looking for an old pair of socks. I can't decide, so I pick the pair I like least (orange with witch faces on them from Halloween two years ago). I walk into the blue room and navigate my way around the huge pile of boxes and furniture until I'm standing in front of the blackboard wall. It's pretty cramped back here, but I think I can manage. I pull a piece of chalk from the box. I make some mental drawings in my head and then begin to work—drawing, erasing with one of the socks, and then redrawing.

I work for about an hour before I hear Mom calling me to help her in the conservatory. No rest for the weary, I guess.

"I'll be down in a minute, Mom. Just finishing something." I finish the last few strokes and stand back (as far as I can without falling over the boxes). "Not bad," I say aloud. I've drawn a new message across the wall: **Welcome to the White House!**

Under the message is a picture of the White House in Washington, D.C. I couldn't remember all the details, and I didn't have a photo of it to copy, so I did the best I could. It's not going to win any awards, but at least you can tell what it is. I could have drawn a picture of our new house, but it wasn't as exciting. Besides, it's a nice play on words, given that our last name is White. Pretty clever, if I do say so myself. The piece of chalk I've been using is merely a little nub now. I put it next to the chalk box and place the Halloween socks on top. I leave the room, turning off the light and closing the door, and head downstairs to help Mom.

That night, Dad and I carry some flattened boxes into the garage. We start bundling them in preparation for recycling pick up later in the week. I ask him why we're not storing them in the attic like we've done before.

"Because I think we're going to be staying here for a while, Lulu," answers Dad.

"Really?" I respond, trying hard to rein in my skepticism.

"This transfer seems a bit more permanent, kitten. If all goes well, there will be some great opportunities down the road for me," says Dad as he puts his arm around my shoulder and steers me back into the house. "Besides, your mom and I would like you to be able to complete as much of your high school career as possible in one place, so we're going to try to stay put. If that's okay with you?"

So, this is it, I think to myself. Our final residence…19 Sycamore Lane.

"Sure. I guess so," I respond, shrugging my shoulders. It doesn't really matter if I want to stay or not. I've wanted to stay every other place we've lived (well, except in first grade when the kids called me *Doo-doo*), but it hasn't made any difference. I don't know why it should make any difference now.

MONDAY, SEPTEMBER 5TH
(LABOR DAY HOLIDAY)

I wake in the morning to the smell of coffee brewing. I guess my parents finally found their coffee maker. That means no more trips to the bagel shop. The coffee maker is plugged in, so, like it or not, this is officially our new home.

As I leave my bedroom, I notice the door to the blue room is slightly ajar. I push open the door and flip on the light. I can't believe my eyes. My masterpiece, all my hard work, is gone. Erased. I race around the pile of boxes and furniture and find the chalk and socks exactly where I left them yesterday. "Welcome to the White House" is completely gone. I stomp out of the room, leaving the light on and the door wide open.

"Why did you erase my drawing?" I demand as I burst into the kitchen. My parents are seated at the breakfast table, with coffee and newspapers in hand.

"Good morning, sweetheart. Sleep well?" asks Mom.

"Good morning, Lulu," says Dad without looking up.

"No, it's not a good morning," I say as I march across the kitchen and clamp my hands down on the back of my empty chair. My knuckles are white because I'm squeezing so hard. "Do you know how long I worked on that drawing? And it was pretty good, too. 'Welcome to the White House.' Get it? 'Cause our last name is White. So why didn't you like it? Tell me!"

"What are you talking about, darling?" asks Mom as she sips her coffee.

"I'm talking about my drawing that I made yesterday on the blackboard wall in the blue room. You erased it, and I want to know why. I worked really hard on it." I stomp my foot and fold my arms across my chest. I'm not leaving here without an answer and, preferably, an apology.

"I didn't erase your drawing, sweetheart. Jim, did you erase it?" asks Mom.

"Huh? What?" replies Dad as he looks up from his newspaper.

"Did you erase my drawing in the blue room?" I demand. This is getting ridiculous.

Dad shakes his head and goes back to his newspaper. "Of course not. I haven't been in that room since the day the movers arrived."

"Then who did it? No one else was in the house yesterday." I throw up my hands, pull out the chair and slump down into it.

"I don't know, darling. Want some breakfast?" asks Mom, going back to her coffee and newspaper.

"Not right now." I stare at my parents for a few moments and then leave the table. I go back to the blue room, grab the nub of chalk that I used yesterday and write one question across the wall: **Who keeps erasing this blackboard?**

I put the piece of chalk back next to the chalk box and leave the room.

* * *

I spend the rest of the day continuing to put my room in order, practicing my music and shopping for school supplies with Mom. After dinner, I set out my clothes for tomorrow and fill up my new backpack with notebooks, pens and pencils. I stand in the bathroom staring at my reflection in the mirror as I brush my teeth. I really don't want to go to school tomorrow. It's not that I hate school. I actually like it, but I hate being the new kid and not knowing anyone. I've moved nine times in fourteen years. I'm always the new kid. Maybe it would be easier to be "new" if I were prettier or at least interesting-looking. But I'm not. I'm profoundly average: average looks, average height, average in almost everyway. The only exception is music, but, in my experience, band geeks aren't usually lauded as cool or popular by the general student population. Perhaps I'll ask Mom if I can dye my hair. I twist a few strands around my finger and study them. It would be better if my hair color was either blond or brown, rather than this in-between color I was born with. A close scrutiny of my face reveals no pimples on the horizon. At least I've got that going for me.

Before I crawl into bed, I check the blackboard. My question is still written large on the wall. Whoever did the erasing — whether it was Mom or Dad, or both — seems to have stopped. I turn off the light and close the door. This time I don't drift off to sleep right away. I lay in bed with the lights off, reading with my flashlight until I can't stay awake any longer. Like it or not, summer has come to an end, and school starts tomorrow. And there's nothing I can do to stop it.

TUESDAY, SEPTEMBER 6TH

When my alarm rings the next morning, I fling off the covers and try to remember my morning routine for school days. It's always confusing the first day back at school after a long summer, and being in a new house where everything is different and unfamiliar certainly doesn't help. I head to the bathroom to start getting ready. On the way there, I notice the door to the blue room is ajar. It was closed last night when I went to bed. I know it was. I open the door the rest of the way, turn on the light and make my way around the boxes and furniture. I stand in front of the blackboard wall and cover my mouth to keep from screaming. My question is still there. It hasn't been erased. The nub of chalk is lying on the floor, and underneath my question is written one word: ME.

I tear out of the room, down the stairs and into the kitchen. I arrive to find Mom clearing away some dishes and Dad putting on his suit jacket.

"Sweetheart, you're not dressed yet? You'd better hurry up. You don't want to be late for your first day of school," says

Mom. She places a bowl of cereal and a glass of orange juice on the table. "Come have your breakfast."

"Have a good day at school, kitten," says Dad. He kisses the top of my head and leaves the kitchen.

"Wait, Dad." I follow him to the front door. "Did you go in the blue room this morning?"

"The blue room? No. Why?" says Dad as he picks up his briefcase.

"So you didn't write anything on the blackboard wall?" I hold my breath.

"No. I'm afraid not. Was I supposed to?" he asks as he puts his keys in his pocket.

"No," I answer. "Just wondering. But, never mind. Have a good day at work." He kisses the top of my head again and leaves the house. I close the door behind him. If it wasn't him, it has to be Mom. I bite my lip and go back to the kitchen. I ask Mom if she went into the blue room.

"No, darling, I haven't been in that room yet today," she replies as she pours herself another cup of coffee. "I need to get in there and sort through those boxes. Maybe I'll get to it this afternoon. Why? Are you looking for something in particular?"

"No," I answer. I eat my breakfast as fast as I can, dress quickly and grab my backpack. Before leaving for school, I stop in the blue room. I stare at the word, ME. It was written with a shaky hand. But whose hand? I grab one of the socks and erase the board. All of it. I close the door, say good-bye to Mom and head for school.

* * *

The first day of school is pretty typical for me. I have trouble finding my classes and get lost several times en route. I have to stand and introduce myself to each class. It's deeply embarrassing the first time I have to do it, but it gets easier as the day goes on. That's largely due to the fact that I seem to have a lot of the same kids in each of my classes. By the time third period starts, most of them have already heard my speech. When the bell rings to signal the lunch period, I follow the crowd to the cafeteria. I don't have anyone to eat lunch with, so I find an empty seat at one of the tables and hope it's not some bully's favorite chair. There haven't been any other "new" students in any of my morning classes, so I stick out like a sore thumb. Most people just stare and don't say anything to me. A few people nod.

I do get stuck in a rather lengthy conversation with one girl at the table, this know-it-all named Chastity Van der Hough. And, yes, she is as annoying as her name sounds. Not in a mean way, though. She simply won't shut up. She decides that it is her personal mission to learn everything about me in the time it takes us to each lunch. I get peppered with questions: Where did I move from? Where else have I lived? Do I play any sports? Do I have any hobbies? Do I have any brothers or sisters? What's my favorite song? Favorite color? Favorite movie? Favorite food? I try to answer each question, but she keeps interrupting me to tell me what her favorites are, what sports she plays and what hobbies she has. By the end of lunch, I've said very little about myself, but I know just about everything I could ever want to know about her. The bell rings, and I'm grateful to have to go back to class.

"Nice meeting you, Tallulah," says Chastity. "See you around." She bounces out of the cafeteria, her ponytail swinging as if it's waving good-bye. I grab my backpack and drag myself up the stairs to my next class. Chastity's interrogation was exhausting, even though she did most of the talking.

For my next to last period of the day, I find myself in chemistry class. I've always liked science, and this classroom is tricked-out with all kinds of equipment. I join the other kids who have congregated in the back of the classroom in a big huddle. Mr. Riddick, who looks a lot like an owl with big, round glasses and bushy grey sideburns, calls out our names and assigns us lab tables and lab partners. I wait patiently for him to call my name and take a seat at a table in the middle of the room. I let out a groan when he calls my lab partner's name.

"Howdy, partner!" says Chastity Van der Hough as she takes a seat on the stool beside me. "This must be kismet. What are the odds that we would become friends during lunch and now be paired up in chemistry class? They must be so tiny, like winning the lottery." She flashes me a smile and plops a sparkly pink notebook on the table.

I want to tell her that the odds can't be as remote as wining the lottery because there are only twenty-four kids in this class, probably only three ninth grade science classes in total and only 75 kids in the entire ninth grade – but I don't. I return her smile, rummage in my backpack for a pencil, and say nothing. Much of class is taken up with Mr. Riddick explaining the rules of the classroom and assigning lab equipment. Whenever Mr. Riddick isn't talking, Chastity is. She simply won't shut up, and she is such a gossip. It's really irritating, especially for me who tends not to talk much at all in school. At the end of class, I look over at Chastity's notebook and she's filled several pages with notes. I'm truly amazed. This girl has managed to pay attention to the teacher and write down everything verbatim, all while talking almost continuously for the entire period. I have to admit that I'm impressed. Obviously, she's smart. Maybe she's not the world's worst lab partner after all.

* * *

"Mom?" I yell as soon as I walk through the front door after school. "Where are you?"

"I'm upstairs," replies Mom. I run up the stairs, throw my backpack on my bed and find Mom in the blue room sorting through boxes. The scene looks much worse than it did this morning. "I don't know where we are going to put all this stuff," says Mom as she pulls an electrical cord from one of the boxes. "What do you think this belongs to?" she asks as she turns the box upside down to show that there's nothing left in there to which it might belong.

I shrug and peer over Mom's shoulder. There's nothing written on the blackboard wall, at least the parts I can see.

"How was school, honey?" asks Mom as she pulls one of Dad's running shoes from a box. "Now where did he pack the other shoe?" Again, all I can do is shrug my shoulders.

"It was fine, Mom," I answer. "I've got a bunch of homework, so can I have a snack and get started on it in the kitchen?"

"Sure, Lulu. Go ahead. You can tell your father and me all about your first day at dinner tonight." Mom opens another large box and groans.

I grab my math book and one of my notebooks from my backpack and disappear into the kitchen. I'm really not in the mood to help Mom with all the unpacking that still needs to be done, so I try to dodge her for the rest of the afternoon. When she emerges from the blue room and comes downstairs, I head upstairs to work on my English homework. She comes back upstairs right before Dad comes home, but I head back down to the kitchen with my chemistry book. So it goes all afternoon, and I make it all the way to dinner without having to unpack a thing.

Dad is more talkative than usual at dinner. Clearly, he's excited about his new job. He and Mom ask me about school.

"Fine," I reply to most of their questions. It's the truth. Today was neither good nor bad. It was purely mediocre. "Nothing much happened," I tell them. "My teachers seem nice enough. They all gave homework, but it's not a crazy amount. No one teased me or picked on me." No one called me *Doo-doo*, fortunately.

"Well, I should hope not," replies Mom. "I'm sure all the kids will like you once they get to know you."

"Right," I answer with a smirk. "I'm sure they're all going to love me." Parents are so naïve sometimes.

I say good night a bit earlier than usual, using the first-day-of-school fatigue syndrome as my excuse. I change into my pajamas, brush my teeth and find myself standing outside the blue room. I'm trying to psych myself up enough to enter. I decided at school today that I need to try to gather some more information before I tell Mom and Dad what's going on, since I'm really not sure what's going on myself. If I'm totally honest – as crazy as it sounds – I think we might have a ghost. I don't really believe in ghosts, or at least I didn't until we moved into this house. But, I don't know…. It's ridiculous, right?

I pace back and forth in front of the door for a while before finally deciding that I'm just going to have to do it. If I don't go in there, I'll never solve this mystery. I turn the doorknob as quietly as possible and slowly open the door. I peek inside and watch for a moment to see if anything moves. Nothing happens. After a couple of deep breaths, I step inside the room and carefully climb over the mess Mom has made. I reach the blackboard wall and discover that my chalk and socks have been moved. I find them in a corner behind some lamps. I decide that Mom must have moved them, because that is the least scary explanation. I take out a new piece of chalk from the box and stand quietly in front of the blackboard. What do I do now? What should I write?

After several minutes, I kneel down and write low on the wall so my parents won't see anything if they open the door and glance in the room. When I'm done, I stand back to survey my work. Satisfied, I put the chalk on the floor right under my one question: **What is your name?**

I turn off the light and close the door. Lying in bed, all I can think about are ghosts, and that's causing me to getting more and more nervous. I'm starting to convince myself that we have one in the house. I don't know what to do. I feel goose bumps spread all over my body. What am I going to tell Mom and Dad? They should know, right? But I can't tell them that the house they just bought has a ghost haunting it. I toss and turn, but I can't shake this growing feeling of dread. What if it tries to harm us? That's it! That's really the most important issue here, isn't it?

I sit straight up in bed. I have to find out if we are in danger. By this time the house is quiet and dark. I sneak back to the blue room, but I hesitate before opening the door. What if there is a ghost in there right now? What will I do if I see it? I'll probably scream bloody murder and run straight out the front door. I swallow hard, open the door and feel along the wall for the light switch. The overhead light blinds me for a second, but I pry my eyes open and look around the room. No sign of ghosts, thankfully.

I add one more question to the blackboard wall: **Are you going to hurt us?**

It's simple and to the point. I place the chalk on the floor under the two questions and notice that my hand is shaking. My heart is also beating a bit faster than usual. What am I doing, trying to communicate with a ghost? And one that might want to do us harm? I turn off the light and close the door. I'm actually dreading what I'll find in the morning. I crawl back into bed and decide to leave a light on in my room tonight as a precaution.

WEDNESDAY, SEPTEMBER 7TH

Morning comes much earlier than I would have liked. Fortunately, I'm still in one piece, and nothing in my room appears to have been disturbed. I race out of my room and stand outside the door to the blue room. My parents are already downstairs, and I'm debating whether to go in and check the blackboard. I'm afraid of what I'll find in there, but I muster as much courage as I can. I swallow hard and open the door. From the doorway, it's hard to tell if anything has been moved since it is such a mess in here. I slowly cross the room, having to climb over boxes and around the piles of stuff. The piece of chalk is on the floor, but it has moved a foot to the right.

I stare at the blackboard. I have answers to my questions. The answers are written in the same shaky penmanship as before: Anastasia. I'm a friend.

I stand there for a moment, frozen, staring at the shaky handwriting. I exhale. I didn't even realize that I had been holding my breath. We're not in danger. That's what's most important. We have a ghost in the house—a real, live (or not so alive) ghost—but at least it's not going to harm us. I grab one of the socks and erase everything from the wall. I just can't look at it anymore, and I certainly don't want Mom or Dad to see it.

I start backing out of the room, but I stop. I'm not sure exactly why I do it, but I walk back to the blackboard wall, grab the piece of chalk and kneel down. Call me impulsive (or insane), but I write a response back to the ghost in small letters so Mom won't notice if she comes in here today: **Good. Me too.**

I leave the chalk and the socks on the floor, turn off the light and leave the room. I get dressed, eat my breakfast and leave for school – all without saying a word to my parents about the ghost.

As soon as I leave the house, I start regretting my decision to write what I wrote. I don't know what came over me. I think I was so relieved that I wanted to write something to make sure the ghost wasn't mad at me for thinking she might hurt my family. Now, I think it may have been a bad idea to write anything at all. Why did I have to write, "**Me too**"? I'm not really sure I want to be a ghost's friend. I guess I should call her Anastasia now that I know her name. Hopefully Anastasia won't take my offer of friendship too seriously.

* * *

I manage to make it to all my classes on time and only get lost once, on my way to third period. At lunch, Chastity waves me over to her table and proceeds to talk me ear off. I think she likes being friends with the new kid, someone who hasn't heard all her stories at least a hundred times before.

"You wouldn't believe what she did to her hair. I mean, what ever possessed her to dye it that color anyway?" asks Chastity, rolling her eyes as if that was the worst thing anyone could do. I shrug my shoulders and take another bite of my sandwich so that I don't have to answer her. She continues to drone on and on, "And I really hate the new uniforms we have to wear. I can't believe someone in the administration approved spending money to buy them. We're going to look ridiculous when we take the field." I'm not sure what she's talking about now, but I admit I haven't been paying very close attention. Chastity leans back in her chair and calls to a girl sitting at the table behind us, "Amber, don't you hate our new uniforms?" I see the girl nod her head. Unfortunately, Amber's mouth is full of food, and she can't reply before Chastity turns back around and launches into another story about her ski trip last winter. I notice that she tends to switch topics without any advance notice, so it's a little hard to follow. She's easily distracted.

When I see her in chemistry class, she's still talking. I would have run out of things to say by now, but not Chastity. Fortunately, I'm starting to learn how to tune her out. It also helps to be a little distracted by the revelation that I have a ghost living in my house. It keeps my mind off the gossip.

I race home from school to find Mom in the blue room sorting through more boxes. Nothing new has been written on the blackboard wall, and empty boxes are blocking the words I wrote this morning. I help Mom unpack for a while, not saying anything about our ghost, and then take my books to the kitchen to start my homework. I finish early today and decide to venture outside for a walk around the neighborhood before I start practicing my music.

In the driveway of the house four doors down on the opposite side of the street, I see two girls playing basketball. They have a hoop attached above the garage door and are taking turns shooting baskets. I recognize one of them from school. She's in my grade but not in any of my classes. I can't remember her name. I don't recognize the other girl who looks older but only by a year or two. In the spirit of trying to be more outgoing, I walk down to where they are and stand watching the girl in my class as she dribbles the ball.

"Hi," I say.

"Shhhh," says the girl from my grade without taking her eyes off the basket. She stands motionless for several moments and then takes her shot. It goes in the basket, making a nice swooshing sound. The other girl chases the ball down and trades places so she can have a turn at the basket.

"Sorry 'bout that," says the girl from my grade. "I was in the zone." She walks over to the sidewalk where I'm standing. "Hey, I know you. You're in ninth grade with me, aren't you? You're the new girl in the gray house down the street, right?"

"Yes. My name is Tallulah. Tallulah White." I smile and put my hands in my pockets since I'm not sure what to do with them. Do fourteen-year olds shake hands when they meet?

The girl nods and smiles. She's very pretty in an athletic, tomboyish sort of way, with golden hair, sky-blue eyes and a dusting of pale freckles across the bridge of her nose. She's about an inch taller than me and doesn't seem to have an ounce of fat on her anywhere.

"Cool. I'm Maisie Bane. That's my sister, Bethany. She's a year ahead of us." Bethany takes her shot and misses. "She's also lousy at basketball," adds Maisie.

"Shut up!" yells Bethany, who is not quite as pretty as her sister. She has the same gorgeous hair and eyes, but her features are not as perfect and she's much more awkward in her movements. "If you hadn't been talking, I would have made that shot."

"Yeah, right. What are you gonna do in an actual game?" teases Maisie.

"Dork!" shouts Bethany as she retrieves the ball and prepares to take another shot. She misses that one, too.

"Want to shoot some hoops with us?" asks Maisie.

"Sure," I answer. "But I've never played, so I really don't know what I'm doing."

"Don't worry. You can't be any worse than Bethany," says Maisie. "Go stand over by that line we've drawn on the driveway. That's the free throw line. Then just take a shot. When you're done you move under the basket to catch the ball that the next person throws, and then you stand out of the way for a shot. We'll go round robin, like that. You, then me, and then Bethany. Okay?"

"I guess so," I say. Bethany tosses me the ball. Well, toss is too nice a word for it. Fires it at me is more like it. She goes and stands under the basket. I bounce the ball in front of me once and then hold it. I study the basket for a moment and shoot. It hits the backboard, but doesn't go anywhere near the basket.

"Not bad. At least you've got the distance. You'll get it. It just takes practice," says Maisie. Bethany fires the ball at her and I move under the basket. Maisie sinks her shot and holds up her hands. "Please, no applause."

"Don't worry," says Bethany as she moves to the free throw line. "No one's giving you any." I toss the ball to Bethany (and I do mean "toss") and stand out of the way. Bethany misses her shot again and swears under her breath. Maisie giggles and tosses me the ball. This goes on for about an hour. Maisie makes most of her shots, Bethany misses almost all of hers, and I actually manage to put few in the basket. My shooting might be improving, but my arms and wrists are aching. Fortunately, Maisie and Bethany are called in to dinner, so I say good-bye and head for home.

"Hey, Tallulah," calls Maisie from her front porch. "Want to walk with us to school tomorrow? We'll come by and get you in the morning when we leave."

"Yeah, that'd be great!" I yell. I wave and run into the house to tell Mom about my two new friends.

* * *

That night, I stand in front of the blackboard wall in my pajamas. I'm not sure what to write. Finally, I decide to start at the beginning. I kneel down and write low to the wall: **My name is Tallulah. Why are you here?**

That should get the ball rolling. I turn off the light and head to bed. I don't know why, but I'm not as nervous about the ghost as I was yesterday. If she says she's a friend, why should I doubt her? She's a ghost, but that doesn't mean she's a liar. Besides, I made two real, live friends today. Three, if you count Chastity (annoying as she is). Why not have a ghost as a friend, too? I decide to keep Anastasia a secret from Mom and Dad, at least for a little while. If it starts getting too weird, then I'll tell them.

THURSDAY, SEPTEMBER 8ᵀᴴ

I wake up a little early because I have two things I need to accomplish this morning. First, I head to the blue room and, with only a split second's hesitation at the door this time, I check to see if Anastasia has written back to me. I am not disappointed. On the wall, in the now-familiar shaky penmanship, is her reply: Nice to meet you, Tallulah. I lived here with my family. This was my room. But I died.

A chill races up my spine. Logically, I know that if Anastasia is a ghost then that means she is dead, but it's quite shocking to see it written in her own handwriting. I wrap my arms around myself, close my eyes and try to take slow, deep breaths to calm myself down. I remind myself that she is supposed to be a friend and won't harm me. I grab the sock and start to erase the blackboard, but I immediately stop. I run back to my room and grab one of my extra notebooks. Something tells me I should be writing this stuff down somewhere since I can't leave it up on the blackboard. It might be important to have a record of everything Anastasia writes. Why? I have no idea. Maybe it will help people believe me if I ever decide to tell anyone. I sit on the floor in front of the blackboard and write down the questions and answers since the beginning a few days ago. I mark the dates next to each entry. And at the top, I give the whole thing a title: "*My Conversations with Anastasia*." I shake my head. No one will ever believe any of this, not in a million years.

I finish erasing the board and head back to my room for the second task of the morning. I need to make sure I'm wearing something kind of cool today. I don't want Maisie and Bethany to think I'm too much of a nerd. Of course, everything in my closet screams, "Nerd!" I pick out the closest things I have to cool, finish getting ready and head downstairs.

I scarf down breakfast and wait by the front door for Maisie and Bethany. The minutes tick by, but there is no sign of them. Finally, Mom says I have to go to school or I'm going to be late. I reluctantly agree. My route to school takes me in the opposite direction of their house, so I can't check to see if they're still home. I have to run most of the way to school and manage to slide into my seat in my first class just as the bell rings. I'm still panting and sweating from my run. It takes me a while to calm down and collect my thoughts. I'm feeling all kinds of things, but mostly anger and embarrassment.

Now, it's possible something terrible happened to Maisie or her sister and they didn't go to school today. They could be at home, sick or hurt. Maybe they're in the hospital. That would be terrible. It would make me feel better about the situation, but it would be terrible for them. Maybe they forgot to pick me up. This was the first time, so it's possible they didn't remember to stop by my house. If that's true, then they have the worst memories of anyone I've ever met. I certainly would have remembered, but it is possible that it was an innocent mistake on their part. This would make me feel a little better, but not as much as if they were in the hospital. I try not to think of the other possibilities, like they were teasing me, because that makes me angrier and even more embarrassed.

I do my best to put it all out of my mind and focus on school, and I'm doing a pretty good job of forgetting about the whole thing until I see Maisie in the lunchroom chatting with a bunch of girls I don't know. Clearly she is not sick. I don't see any casts on her arms or legs, and she's not wearing any bandages from head trauma. I'm so flustered that I buy a drink and take my lunch outside. I can't muster the courage to go over to Maisie and confront her, at least not in front of a bunch of people I don't know. I'll just ignore her. If she says anything about it, I'll say I left early and forgot all about her offer – so sorry if she was waiting for me. I'll turn it around and make it seem like I was the one who slighted her. That's it. Problem solved. I pick at my lunch and end up putting it back in my backpack. I've lost my appetite.

When the bell rings to end my last class, I race out of school and head home as quickly as I can. I don't want to run into Maisie or Bethany, so I make sure I'm one of the first people out the door. I make it home without seeing them. Of course, by now I'm starving, so the first order of business is to have a snack. My lunch has been totally squashed in the bottom of my backpack, so I have to toss it out. What used to be a sandwich now looks like a pancake, the pretzels are nothing but crumbs, and the grapes resemble something from a horror movie. I fix myself a fresh sandwich and a glass of milk, and I pull out my math book. Mom has made chocolate chip cookies, so I help myself to one before going upstairs to my room to finish my homework. If I move my desk chair over to the left a little bit, I have a view of Maisie's house through the trees. I can see her and her sister playing basketball. They both appear to be healthy and in one piece. I glare at them and try to finish my homework. It takes me longer than usual since I'm constantly glancing out the window. Some boy rides his bike up to their house and joins them. They appear to be having fun, and this makes me fume even more. I'm hoping for rain. Hail would be even better. Softball-size hail, that's what we need right now.

After dinner, I watch television with my parents, but I can't enjoy it. My feelings are still too bruised. I say good night and go upstairs to get ready for bed. Before turning in, I sit on the floor in the blue room in front of the blackboard. I've been so preoccupied with being snubbed by Maisie that I sort of forgot about Anastasia. But, now it's back to business. I need more information this time, so I'm going to have to ask some more questions: **When did you die? How did you die? How old were you? Where is the rest of your family? Why are you still here? Can I help you?**

I hesitate with the last one. I'm a bit nervous about a ghost asking me for help. What if she wants me to do something

38

terrible? I erase the last question, but then I change my mind and rewrite it.

I can't fall asleep. I keep thinking I hear sounds coming from the blue room. I'm not about to go in there and check. It's one thing to have a ghost as a pen pal. It's quite another to actually come face to face with her!

FRIDAY, SEPTEMBER 9TH

I get out of bed even before my alarm rings and make sure that my parents are both downstairs before slipping into the blue room. Anastasia has written back to me. I open my notebook and copy down the questions and answers:

1. **When did you die?** I died 10 years ago.
2. **How did you die?** I fell. Long story.
3. **How old were you?** I was 16.
4. **Where is the rest of your family?** They moved away after I died.
5. **Why are you still here?** I'm needed here.
6. **Can I help you?** No, but maybe I can help you.

I scribble away, but I'm not sure what to make of the last answer. How can she help me? And it's sad that she stays here even though her family is gone. Why does she think she's needed here? Who could possibly need her to haunt this house? I certainly don't, but I won't be impolite and tell her that. I finish writing and grab one of the socks to erase the board when I notice some more writing. Behind the large box on which the socks had been placed, I see Anastasia's handwriting. I move the box out of the way. The writing is bigger and bolder than the rest: **Stay away from Maisie Bane!** Under the warning, I find the chalk broken in half.

I stop breathing. I'm frozen to the floor and staring at the warning. How does she know about Maisie? Up until this moment, I had assumed that Anastasia stays in the blue room. This is where she communicates with me, so this must be where she is – nowhere else. But clearly that is wrong. She could be anywhere. And, she's been spying on me. Goosebumps run up my arms and I force myself to start breathing again, and I erase the warning and the rest of the writing. I add the line about Maisie to my notebook. Now what do I do?

I don't eat much breakfast, and Dad heads to work while I'm still playing with my cereal. Mom is giving a couple of music lessons this morning, so she's racing around tidying up the house and doesn't notice that I've barely touched my food. I leave for school, constantly checking over my shoulder for Maisie and her sister. I make it to school, only to find them hanging out on the front steps. I'm not sure whether to take Anastasia's warning seriously, but I err on the side of caution and enter the school through the side entrance. It means I have to walk much farther to my locker and then back again to my first class, but it seems the safest course of action at the moment.

I manage to avoid Maisie all day at school, which is much harder than I thought it would be. Normally I don't see that much of her during the day since she's not in any of my classes.

But today, she's everywhere. Every time I turn around, there she is. It takes some creative footwork, but I steer clear of her. I head to the library after school for about an hour to do some homework, but mainly to hide out. Then I head home, assuming she will be long gone. And she is. There is no sign of her until I turn down my street. As usual, she is in her driveway with her sister Bethany playing basketball. Don't they ever do their homework? Don't they ever stay inside their house? I walk as quickly as I can down the sidewalk until I reach my yard. As I'm crossing it with my head down, I hear Maisie's voice.

"Tallulah! Hey, Tallulah! Want to play?" She's waving at me with one hand and dribbling the basketball with the other.

"Can't," I shout back. "Have homework."

"But it's Friday! Come over and play with us," yells Maisie.

"Sorry," I reply. I run across the lawn and straight into the house through the front door. I close it and lock it behind me.

"Sweetheart? Is that you?" asks Mom. She has to yell over the noise emanating from the music room. It sounds like someone is torturing a cat in there.

"Yes," I yell to her. I drop my backpack and lean against the front door. My heart is thumping loudly in my chest. This is crazy. I don't even know why I should stay away from Maisie. Other than the fact that she stood me up the other day on our way to school, she hasn't done anything wrong. Anastasia's warning is making me paranoid.

"How was school?" asks Mom as she enters the foyer.

"Fine," I answer. "Sounds like a violin lesson."

"Does it? Really?" Mom smiles and winks at me.

I open my mouth to tell her everything, but I don't know where to begin or what to say. It all sounds crazy, the explanations swirling around in my head. I sigh and pick up my backpack.

"I'm going to have a snack and start my homework," I tell her, and I start to shuffle towards the kitchen. I know it's Friday, but I don't know what else to do. I can't go outside, and Mom doesn't like me practicing my music while she's giving a lesson. I opt for doing homework because I need to keep myself busy, or I'll go insane.

"That's fine, darling, but don't spoil your appetite. We're going out to dinner tonight as soon as your father gets home," says Mom as she heads back into her conservatory.

I grab an apple and sit down at the table with my chemistry book. What a day. I'm exhausted from all the ducking and weaving – and worrying. I can't keep this up. I have to find out why Anastasia wrote that warning.

* * *

I go to dinner with my parents at the pizzeria in town. Normally, I would be excited to have pizza, but I have too much on my mind. I think my parents might be starting to suspect something is wrong with me. They ask me a million questions, especially about school. Okay, it might not be a million, but it certainly feels like it. Let's just say it's more than the usual number. Mom keeps feeling my forehead and asking me if I'm not feeling well.

"I'm fine, really," I lie. "Just not very hungry tonight." Of course, that is the wrong thing to say, because Mom reaches over and feels my forehead again. I'm never "not very hungry" for pizza. It's my absolute favorite food. She knows if I'm not stuffing my face with it then there must be something wrong. I can't tell her that my head is spinning and there is a giant knot in my stomach because a ghost told me to stay away from our neighbor. That wouldn't go over well. Instead, I smile and try my best not to look tense and freaked out.

We walk home, and I don't say much. Mom and Dad insist that I stay up and watch a movie with them. Mom selects *Casablanca*, again. I've seen it so many times I could act in it myself. I agree to watch the movie, but the minute it's over I'm heading upstairs to write to Anastasia.

SATURDAY, SEPTEMBER 10ᵀᴴ

I wake up the next morning on the sofa still wearing my school clothes from yesterday. I fell asleep at some point during the movie and my parents threw a blanket over me and left me here all night. I stand and stretch. I catch a glimpse of myself in the mirror that hangs over the fireplace mantle. My hair is practically standing straight up off my head, and I have deep pillow creases across my right cheek. Lovely. Worse than that is the realization that I've missed my opportunity to ask Anastasia some more questions. I head upstairs to the blue room and find Mom already sorting through boxes. I breathe a sigh of relief that I didn't write anything to Anastasia, because Mom most certainly would have seen her answers before I had a chance to erase them.

I go back downstairs and find Dad in the kitchen. I pour myself a bowl of cereal and sit down at the table as Dad's cell-phone starts ringing. He takes the call.

"That's terrible," says Dad to some mystery caller. "Yes, I know. Well, I think I can help. Or, rather, I believe my daughter can." Dad winks at me. I scowl at him as well as I can with my mouth full of cereal. "What time do we need to be there? No problem. See you then." Dad hangs up and smiles at me.

"What?" I ask. This won't be good. I can tell by the ridiculous grin on his face.

"Lulu, ever heard of the Junior Football League?" asks Dad.

"Nope," I answer and spoon another bite of cereal into my mouth.

"Well," begins Dad. "It's a recreational football league for kids from several of the local towns. It's a big deal here, evidently. Anyway, the Junior Football League Opening Day is today, and my company is one of the primary sponsors. It appears that the kid who was supposed to play the national anthem at the opening ceremony broke two of his fingers yesterday at football practice, and they need someone to fill in last minute," Dad explains, still grinning from ear to ear.

"So?" I say. I know what's coming.

"So," says Dad. "I might have mentioned at the office that you play several instruments. That was one of my colleagues calling to ask if you could fill in."

"Oh, Dad. No, no, no," I whine. "I really don't want to do it. Can't they find someone else?"

"Well, kitten, I already told them you would," says Dad, still smiling. "It would really help me out – and help out my company. And I know you can play the national anthem. I've heard you play it hundreds of times. You'll be fantastic. It'll be fun, you'll see. We need to leave in about thirty minutes, so finish your breakfast and get ready." Dad drains that last of the coffee in his mug.

"Exactly what instrument do you want me to play?" I ask.

"I think the trumpet would be best, don't you?" he answers. He tucks his newspaper under his arm and leaves the kitchen. I knew he was going to say the trumpet. He loves it, but it's my least favorite.

I put my cereal bowl in the sink and climb the stairs to my room to get ready. I make a pit stop in the blue room to complain to Mom about what Dad is making me do, but I get no sympathy from her. She's so excited that she decides to come with us. Half an hour later we are in the car, trumpet case on the seat next to me, heading to the League's athletic fields. We arrive with no time to spare.

"Just play nice and loud, Lulu," says Dad as he kisses my forehead. I look around. Fortunately, I don't think anyone heard him call me that.

"Right, Dad" I reply as I walk out onto the field when the announcer calls my name. I line up behind the microphone and let it rip. Dad wanted loud, so that's exactly what I give him, plus a couple of flourishes thrown in for dramatic effect. When I finish, I can hear Dad's whistle over the cheers of the crowd. I feel the blood rush to my cheeks, and I tuck my chin as I speed walk to the sideline.

"Sweetheart, don't hide your face," says Mom as I approach. "That was really good. You should be very proud."

"I was a little sharp at the beginning and I lost the tempo twice," I complain.

"Yes," agrees Mom. "But you really made it your own, and you should be proud of your performance." Mom puts her arm around me and squeezes. She's always good about giving encouragement along with the constructive criticism.

"Wonderful, kitten," says Dad. He scoops my face in his hands and kisses my forehead again. "That was just perfect." I can always count on Dad to love anything I play. He has absolutely no musical talent whatsoever, so he thinks everything I do is great.

"Thanks, Dad," I say. "Can we go home now?"

"Not yet, kiddo," answers Dad. "I need to make the rounds and shake a few hands. Why don't you watch some of the games? Your mom and I will come find you when it's time to leave." Dad hands me some money for the concession stand and walks over to a couple of men standing in the end zone.

"Excuse me," says a man approaching Mom and me. "Excuse me, Miss White." This stranger knows my name, which freaks me out. I take a step back. He nods his head at me. "Madam," he says to Mom, nodding his head at her as well. He turns to face me. "I just heard your performance. Wonderful, just wonderful! My name is Patrick Murphy, and I'm the music teacher at the local school." He shakes my hand enthusiastically and then does the same to Mom. "Is there any chance you are a new student there? I haven't seen you before."

"Go Mongooses," I say with a half-hearted fist pump.

"Yes," answers Mom. "We just moved to the area a week ago." She smiles sweetly at him and puts her arm around my shoulder.

"Excellent!" he says. "Well, I'd like to invite you to join the school orchestra. We have band class the last period of the day, so it may mean rearranging your schedule a little. What class do you have last period?"

"It's just a study period," I say.

"Wonderful! Then we won't have to rearrange anything else." Mr. Murphy smiles and throws up his hands. "But listen to me! I haven't even asked if you'd be interested in the orchestra." I shrug my shoulders. In a school of only a thousand kids, I can't imagine the orchestra is very good. He scratches his chin. "Well, do you like playing the trumpet?"

"It's okay," I answer. "But it's not my favorite."

"So you play more than one instrument, then. My, my, that is lucky for us. What is your favorite, Tallulah?" He folds his arms across his chest and presses his lips together to try to hide his enthusiasm.

"The piano is my favorite. Then flute. Then clarinet and trumpet," I reply. "I like the violin, but I'm not very good at it yet. I also really like the pipe organ, but I only recently started taking lessons from Mom." Mr. Murphy nods and fights the smile growing across his face.

"I see," he says. "That's very impressive." He smiles at Mom. "So you're a musician, as well?"

"Yes, sir," answer Mom. "I play a variety of instruments and have played with several orchestras. I'll be giving music lessons at my home, if you have any students you might wish to refer." She smiles again sweetly.

"Oh, you and I definitely need to chat," says Mr. Murphy nodding. "But, back to you, Tallulah. Have you ever played the piccolo?" I shake my head. "Well, would you be willing to give it a try?"

I look up at Mom, who smiles and raises an eyebrow. "I don't know. Maybe," I say and shrug my shoulders again.

"Well, I need a piccolo in our orchestra. I've had a few of the flute players give it a try, but none of them has really taken to it. Given your considerable musical talent, I think you may be more successful at picking it up."

I bite my lip. I'm not sure I want to take on any more instruments. It's already so time consuming to practice the ones I have now.

Mr. Murphy claps his hands together. "I'm willing to make you a deal," he says. "If you agree to join the school orchestra and sign up for band class – and you agree to give the piccolo a try – I can arrange for you to have access to a pipe organ. You could resume your lessons with your mother. Does that sound good to you?"

"Really?" I say. I can feel myself grinning from ear to ear.

"Absolutely. You have my word," says Mr. Murphy. "I'm the music director at St. Michael's church in town. We have a beautiful organ. I can arrange some practice time for you... if we have a deal?"

I look up at Mom. She nods and says, "I think that sounds like a very good deal, sweetheart. You can use my piccolo, the one I played when we lived in St. Louis. It's in good condition, and I can give you some lessons to help you get up to speed quickly. What do you say?"

I don't have to think about it too long. Any chance to get access to a pipe organ is worth having to learn the stupid piccolo. "Alright, I'll do it."

Mr. Murphy shakes my hand again. He's so excited that he nearly wrenches my arm out of its socket. "Fantastic!" he says. "Come to the band room on Monday for your last period of the day. It's on the second floor at the south end of the school. I'll talk to your guidance counselor and make all the arrangements to get your schedule switched to add band class in place of study hall. I think you're really going to like the piccolo, Tallulah. I think this is going to be very successful for you and me both." He smiles at me and then hands Mom a business card. "Give me a call at the church, and we'll make arrangements regarding the organ." He waves at us as he walks away.

"I'm very proud of you, honey," says Mom as she squeezes my shoulder. "I'm going to go find your father. Why don't you walk around, see if any of your new friends are here?" She kisses me on the cheek and disappears into the crowd. I roll my eyes. I'd have to have friends in order for them to be here. Anastasia is a ghost, so that's not going to help right now. I'm not so sure I should count Maisie amongst my friends at the moment. And Chastity has no reason to be here since she doesn't play football (she only plays lacrosse) and she's an only child. I know this because she has told me both facts at least a dozen times since I met her just five days ago.

I buy a drink and roam around the grounds, checking out the various games underway. I finally decide to watch the littlest kids play, and I pick a seat at the end of a row in the bleachers. The little kids' games are called "Tiny Tykes," according to a rather large and boisterous woman sitting next to me. For half an hour I watch a bunch of five-year olds, all wearing helmets and jerseys that are several sizes too big, bump into each other and trip over their own feet — none of which looks much like football. It's the funniest thing I've seen in a while. The game ends, and I clap and cheer along with the other spectators. The next teams to take the field are older. Their uniforms fit better, and they seem to know more about what they are supposed to be doing on the field. At least they are consistently running in the right direction. Consequently, they are much less entertaining.

"Hey!" I feel a tap on my arm. I look around to find a girl about my age standing next to the bleachers and staring up at me. She has long, curly, flame-colored hair and bright green eyes.

"Me?" I ask, not sure what she could possibly want. Perhaps she's a fan of my trumpet playing.

"Are you the girl who just moved into the grey house on Sycamore Lane? Number 19?" she asks. I nod.

"Bad things happen to kids in that house," says the flame-haired girl. Her eyes are open so wide that I'm afraid they'll pop out of their sockets. She clamps her hand on my arm. "Watch out! Don't believe her, not one word. She's trouble. She'll hurt you. Do you hear me? She's going to try to hurt you!"

"Come on, Cee!" yells a little boy in a blue and white football uniform. He was one of the kids I saw playing in the Tiny

Tykes match. He runs up to the girl and tugs on the bottom of her shirt. "Dad says we have to go now. Em needs to go home and rest."

"Okay," says the girl. She takes his hand and leads him away.

The little boy looks back over his shoulder. I hear him ask, "Who is that girl?" I can't hear his sister's response.

"Tallulah!" Mom is waving at me from the other side of the bleachers. I wave back and grab my trumpet case. As I scramble off the bleachers, I look around to try to find the flame-haired girl, but she has vanished. My heart thumps loudly in my chest. Why do I keep getting these crazy warnings? Who was that girl and how did she know I moved into the house at 19 Sycamore Lane? She said bad things happen to the kids who live there. How does she know that? And who is going to try to hurt me? Does she mean Maisie?

I take a few steps, and then it hits me. I stumble and drop my trumpet case. Is it possible that she was warning me about Anastasia? Is the ghost the reason bad things happen to kids who live in my house? What if the ghost I thought was my friend has been lying to me, trying to throw me off track by making me afraid of Maisie? What if Anastasia is the one who has plans to hurt me? My knees buckle and I slump to the ground. Mom comes rushing over to me.

"Sweetheart, are you okay? What's wrong?" She feels my forehead. I've broken out in a cold sweat despite the heat of the day. "Lulu, you're as white as a sheet. Maybe we should get you to a doctor." People are starting to gather around us. Dad pushes threw the crowd and kneels down beside me.

"What's wrong, kitten? What happened?" he asks as he strokes my hair.

"Nothing. I'm fine," I reply. "I don't need a doctor. I just want to go home." And then I realize that home is probably the worst place for me right now. Frantically, I try to think of somewhere, anywhere, that we can go other than home, but I can't. Mom and Dad put me into the backseat of the car, and we drive to our house.

When we arrive at 19 Sycamore Lane, I swallow hard and exit the car. Cautiously, I follow my parents inside and stand in the foyer, not sure what to do next. Dad takes the trumpet case out of my hand, and Mom helps me up the stairs.

"I want you to rest," says Mom as she leads me into my bedroom. "Let me get the thermometer. If you have a fever, we are going straight to the emergency clinic." Much to Mom's surprise, my temperature is perfectly normal. Dad brings me a glass of orange juice, a turkey sandwich and two chocolate chip cookies, but I'm too frightened to eat. They insist that I take a nap. I pull the comforter up over my head and shut my eyes as tightly as I can, but I can't sleep. Once I'm sure Mom and Dad are out of earshot, I sneak the notebook out of my desk drawer and review the *Conversations* to date. Nothing Anastasia wrote to me on the blackboard wall would indicate that she's trying to harm me. So why was the flame-haired girl so adamant that I was in danger? My head is throbbing. I bury it under my pillows and eventually fall asleep.

I wake a couple of hours later. No signs of a ghost anywhere, and I'm still very much alive and in one piece, thankfully. I find

Mom hard at work in the blue room. Fortunately, nothing is written on the blackboard wall. Just standing in the blue room is making my heart race. Mom gives me a reprieve from unpacking duty and sends me downstairs. I practice the piano for a while and then curl up with Dad on the sofa to watch television until dinner. I stay up as late as I can, hanging out with my parents until they shoo me upstairs to bed. The door to the blue room is open. I close it and back away. I don't write any questions for Anastasia. I think it's safer to leave her alone. Hopefully she'll do the same with me.

SUNDAY, SEPTEMBER 11TH

I wake the next day to the smell of bacon. The door to the blue room is wide open. I stand in the doorway and look around. Mom made some progress yesterday, but the room is still a mess. More importantly, Anastasia hasn't written anything. I breathe a sigh of relief. Maybe she won't try to communicate with me anymore. The giant knot in my stomach makes me think I won't be that lucky.

I confine myself to the house today. I don't want to go outside, in case Maisie sees me. I'm still not sure if I should be afraid of her as well. She hasn't tried to hurt me, at least not physically. I also steer clear of the blue room. I don't want to go anywhere near the blackboard wall. I read the *Conversations* in my notebook over and over again until I can recite them from memory. I keep coming back to Anastasia's offer to "help" me and her claim that she is "a friend". Has she been lying? Trying to trick me? I wish I knew whom I could trust. The anxiety is giving me a perpetual stomachache.

I spend the day practicing my music. Mom gives me a very lengthy lesson on the piccolo, which goes reasonably well. I don't think it will be too long before I can become proficient at it. I also put in practice time with each of my other instruments, playing until my fingers ache and my lips are sore. I finish my homework for Monday, I rearrange my closet and refold all the clothes in my dresser. I even help Mom with some housework. I hate cleaning the bathrooms, but I volunteered today just to keep my mind off my dilemma. Nothing refocuses your attention liking scrubbing toilets. I stay busy and make it through the day without anything bad happening to me. However, I'm exhausted. I can't keep this up. Mom and Dad will get suspicious if I clean the bathrooms every day just to avoid any interaction with Anastasia and Maisie.

During dinner, I find myself running through the *Conversations* in my head. I need some answers. I need to be brave for once in my life. I wash the dishes and then I head straight upstairs, telling my parents I have to finish some homework. I don't really, but I do need some time in front of the blackboard. I have to figure out what's going on around here. My well-being (and my sanity) depends on it. So, first things first. I need Anastasia to give me an explanation of her warning. Maybe her answer will give me some clue as to whether she's been lying to me.

I stand in front of the blackboard wall for a long time, not knowing what to write. I don't want to make Anastasia mad. Right now, she doesn't know that I talked to the flame-haired girl at the football game. At least I don't think she knows. I decide that it's best to carry on as if nothing has happened, as if I've received no other warnings. I gather my courage and write:

Why should I stay away from Maisie? She seems nice and friendly. Why don't you like her? Your warning scared me.

I close the blue room door, brush my teeth and crawl into bed. I stay up reading for a while. I'm about to turn off the light and go to sleep when I hear the sound of chalk on the blackboard. I feel myself go cold, and my heart leaps into my throat. I leave the light on and pull my comforter up over my head to try to drown out the sounds. It doesn't work.

MONDAY, SEPTEMBER 12TH

I wake in the morning, and everything in my room is as it should be. Before getting dressed, I head to the blue room. Anastasia was busy last night. In shaky letters, she has answered my questions: Maisie is not your friend. She will only get you in trouble. It happened to Maryanne and Caroline. Don't trust her.

As for my statement about her warning scaring me, she wrote: I did not mean to scare you. I am only trying to help. I don't want to see you get hurt like the others.

"Holy cow!" I yell. I quickly cover my mouth and glance over my shoulder, waiting to see if Mom or Dad will come running in to check on me. I don't hear anything, so they must both be downstairs. I remove my hand from my mouth and realize I'm biting down pretty hard on my bottom lip. I stare at Anastasia's handwriting.

Her warning bears a striking resemblance to the warning from the flame-haired girl. But can I trust Anastasia? Is she lying to me, trying to confuse me? I read her responses several more times. Who are Maryanne and Caroline? Who are the "others"? I force myself to stop biting my lip before I draw blood. Before I decide to trust Anastasia, I'll need to do some investigating on my own. In the meantime, I'll try to avoid Maisie just to be safe.

After breakfast, I walk to school, constantly looking over my shoulder to make sure Maisie and Bethany aren't around. I make it without any sightings of them and head straight for the library. I've got a good twenty minutes before my first class, and I think I should start my investigations with the librarian, Mrs. Thistlewhyte. Being the librarian, she probably knows most, if not all, of the kids in this school. Hopefully she won't get suspicious if I start asking questions. There are a couple of kids in the library studying or doing research, but I don't recognize any of them. I find the librarian reshelving books in the back of the library.

"Excuse me, Mrs. Thistlewhyte," I whisper as I approach her. She's bent over a cart of books.

"Yes, young lady," she responds as she stands up. She grabs her lower back and groans a little.

"Here, let me help," I offer. I bend down and hand her some of the books from the bottom of the cart.

"Thank you, my dear. My back can't take all that bending over this early in the morning." Mrs. Thistlewhyte studies the Dewey Decimal coding on each spine and files them accordingly on the shelves. We reshelve about ten books before I ask her a question.

"Mrs. Thistlewhyte, I'm new to the area. I moved here a couple of days before school started, and I was wondering if you happened to know if there are any girls named Maryanne and Caroline in this school?" I hand her another set of books and wait for her reply.

"Well, there are quite a few Carolines and even a couple Maryannes. Do you know their last names?" she asks as she moves farther down the rows of books.

"I'm afraid I don't. I think they may have known each other. Maybe they were friends." I don't know why I think this. It's just a hunch. There was something about the way Anastasia wrote their names together on the board. It just makes me think that they were linked in some way.

Mrs. Thistlewhyte stops reshelving and looks at me, studying me up and down. "We did have a set of twins named Caroline and Maryanne. Let's see…." She moves to the end of the aisle and turns the corner. I follow her to a bookshelf near the check-out desk. She selects a tall thin yearbook from the shelf and starts flipping pages. "Yes, here they are: Caroline and Maryanne Dent," she says. "They moved, I believe, so they don't go to this school anymore, but they were in the eighth grade last year." She hands me the yearbook and points to two photos on the page. The girls look identical, with long, curly, flame-colored hair and bright green eyes.

"Really?" I say, trying to keep my voice calm. "That's very helpful, Mrs. Thistlewhyte. Thank you!" She smiles and walks back across the library to her cart. I place the yearbook on the shelf and race out of the library. I can feel myself starting to hyperventilate, so I burst through the side door to the school and out into the open schoolyard. I take in huge gulps of fresh air, willing my heart to stop pounding in my chest. I walk slowly up and down the sidewalk for a few minutes to collect myself before I have to go back in and find my first class.

I cover my face with my hands and try to concentrate. The girl who approached me at the football field was either Maryanne or Caroline Dent. That would be weird enough on its own. What really makes my blood run cold, however, is the realization that I'm living in her old house. I'm sleeping in her old bedroom.

I know this because the family we bought our house from was named Dent. I remember Dad saying something about them when he and Mom were getting ready to sign the contract. I know they had twin girls, and I took their lavender bedroom when we moved in. I never learned their first names or how old they were at the time. I just knew they were older than their brother, who had the blue room. The kid in the blue and white football uniform must be their little brother.

I reach back into my brain trying to recall the details from Saturday. I remember the little boy calling the girl, "Cee." He also said "Em needs to go home and rest." What if he really said, "C" and "M" – like their initials. Maybe his nicknames for them are "C" and "M." Caroline and Maryanne!

That's whom Anastasia was talking about. It has to be. But how were they hurt? And who hurt them? Was it Maisie, or was it Anastasia?

* * *

When the bell for lunch rings, I enter the lunchroom and look for Chastity. Given her propensity for gossip, I'm willing to bet that she can help me with my investigations. Unfortunately, she is nowhere to be found. As I scan the lunchroom, Maisie looks up from her lunch. She stares at me and eventually a sly smile creeps across her face. I take a few steps backward and bump into a rather large boy, who proceeds to curse at me for making him spill his drink. I apologize to him, make a quick exit and take my lunch outside. I'm too nervous to eat much, and I suffer in silence until chemistry class.

Once we get our instructions from our teacher, we break up into our pairs to perform today's experiment. Chastity is in good voice today. She launches right into what so-and-so did this morning to who-knows-who right before school. I bite my tongue, waiting for an opening. When she pauses to take a breath, I jump in.

"Hey, Chastity," I begin slowly, pretending I'm reading something in our textbook. "Do you remember twin sisters named Maryanne and Caroline Dent? I think they went to school here last year."

"Sure, everyone remembers them," she says, her eyes getting big. She leans in closer and whispers, "Such a shame, what happened to them. They were really nice girls. Both were in chorus and in the drama club. Really sweet." She shakes her head and looks at our test tubes to find the one we need next. And, for the first time since I've known her, she's quiet. She says nothing for several minutes.

I can't take it anymore and blurt out, "What happened to them!?!" Most of the class hears me, and my teacher, Mr. Riddick, has to tell me to stop talking and get to work. It's mildly embarrassing, but a little embarrassment is worth it to get some answers.

Chastity raises an eyebrow. "Alright, don't get upset. I think they're fine now, but that's why they moved away. They don't go to school here anymore. I forget where they moved to. Somewhere near by. Where was it?" Chastity taps her chin with her pencil to help her think.

"It doesn't matter where they moved to," I whisper. "What happened to them?"

She puts her pencil down and turns to me, looking very serious. "Oh, they had this terrible accident. They were playing with some other kids in their neighborhood. They were all riding bikes. You're new so you may not know the neighborhood, but it's up the hill behind the school here. Have you been up there? There are some really beautiful houses on the hill. There's this one house that is my favorite. In Spring, it has hundreds of tulips that sprout up all across the front yard. It's really stunning."

"Chastity!" I hiss through clenched teeth. "Please focus. You were telling me about Maryanne and Caroline Dent, remember?"

"Okay, okay. I'm getting to them," she says. She sighs and shifts in her seat. "There's this one street on the other side of that neighborhood that is really steep. It's called Crows Nest Lane, for obvious reasons. Some kids like to ride their bikes down it, but it's dangerous because it's so steep and it ends at Cooper Street. You know, the main road that comes around the front of the school and into town?" I nod my head.

Chastity picks a test tube and pours the contents into the beaker. I stir. She continues, "They got new bikes for Christmas last year. You know, the kind with hand brakes, not the brakes on the pedals. And they were playing with a bunch of kids in their neighborhood. Apparently, some of the kids were riding their bikes down Crows Nest Lane, and someone dared Maryanne and Caroline to do it, too. They must have caved to the pressure, because both girls decided to do it – together. They got on their bikes at the top and road down the hill. Well, something happened to their bikes because the brakes wouldn't work and they couldn't stop. Caroline managed to steer her bike over to the side of the road. She hit the curb and went flying into someone's yard. She landed on the grass, but she broke her arm and a couple of ribs. She was pretty bruised, too. Maryanne wasn't so lucky. She didn't try to swerve or anything. She went flying down Crows Nest Lane, right through the stop sign and into the middle of Cooper Street."

"Ladies," says Mr. Riddick. He is standing right behind us. "Less talking and more working, please. I don't want to have to tell you again."

"Yes, sir," I say and go back to stirring the contents of our beaker. Once he is on the other side of the room, I whisper, "Go on. What happened to Maryanne?"

Chastity glances over her shoulder and leans closer. "She was hit by a car."

"What?" I gasp. I cover my mouth so quickly that I drop my pencil. I scramble off my stool to retrieve it. Mr. Riddick is glaring at me from across the room. I hold up the pencil and mouth the word, "Sorry." He shakes his head and turns away. I hop back up onto the stool.

Chastity nods her head at me, eyes wide. "There was a car coming. She couldn't stop and neither could the car. It hit her and she went flying over the handlebars, hit the windshield of the car and landed on the sidewalk on the other side of Cooper Street. The ambulance came. There was blood everywhere. She was in the hospital for months. Their parents took them out of school and home-schooled them for the rest of the year."

"That's terrible. Was Maryanne okay? After she recovered?" I realize my hands are trembling, and I'm in danger of dropping my pencil again.

"Sort of. I hear she walks with a bit of a limp now, and someone said her head injuries have made her a little, well... slow, if you know what I mean," says Chastity. She's shaking her head as she grabs the next test tube and adds its contents to the beaker.

"Wow," I whisper. "That's awful. Really, really awful. Those poor girls." I realize that the flame-haired girl who gave me the warning didn't walk with a limp, so she must have been Caroline Dent.

"They claimed it was sabotage," says Chastity as she makes some notes in her notebook.

"What do you mean?" I ask.

Chastity glances over her shoulder again. "Rumor was that the twins claimed their brakes had been tampered with, like the brake cables had been partially cut so that they would break when squeezed really hard. They claimed it was done by someone who goes to school here."

"Who?" I manage to not yell out, but it was close. It came out as a very loud whisper.

"Maisie Bane," whispers Chastity. Her voice is so quiet that it's hard to hear, but I definitely heard Maisie's name. "It was never proven, though. The girls said they thought Maisie was the culprit, because she was the one who convinced them to go down the hill. They said she even threatened to hurt their little brother if they didn't do it. Maisie denied the whole thing and wandered around school with red, puffy eyes for days after it happened. She said Caroline and Maryanne were her best friends. She tried to visit them in the hospital, but she wasn't allowed to see them."

I sit back on the stool and stare at the beaker. This must be what Anastasia was trying to tell me. "Does anyone think Maisie was involved?"

Chastity glances around again. "I do," she says and nods her head. "Some people don't, but I've known Maisie since kindergarten. We were in the same class. I saw her hit a boy over the head with a wooden truck. He needed fifteen stitches. Or was it sixteen? I can't remember." She taps her chin again with her pencil. "We had the same pediatrician, Dr. Bhandari."

"Chastity, please!" I beg. "Focus!"

"Calm down," she says, shaking her head. "Anyway, Maisie told the teacher that she and this boy were playing, and he started chasing her. She threw the truck at him in self-defense to get him to stop, because she was afraid he was going to hurt her. But that wasn't the truth. I saw it. She bashed him over the head with the truck. And for no apparent reason. I told the teacher, and she got in trouble. My mom wouldn't let me play with her after that. She was transferred to a different kindergarten class because the boy's parents made such a stink about it." Chastity hands me a test tube. "Here, your turn."

I read the instructions in our book and then pour the contents into the beaker. Chastity stirs.

"There have been other incidents, too," she whispers. "Nothing that could be proven, of course. She gets accused of doing bad things but never gets in trouble. She's never caught actually doing anything. I think she learned that lesson in kindergarten."

"What else has she been accused of?" I ask. Chastity is on a roll. I knew she was the right person to ask.

"Let's see," she taps her chin with her pencil. "There was a girl in second grade who got a concussion from falling off the monkey bars. She said it was Maisie's fault, but she couldn't prove it. In sixth grade, a boy broke his leg riding his skateboard down Crows Nest Lane. He claimed that Maisie threw some rocks in the road, and he hit them. Fortunately, he didn't go into the intersection at Cooper Street, but he did hit a parked car. Again, no one saw her do anything. I'm sure there have been other things, but that's all I can remember right now."

"That's terrible. Do you really think she did all those things?" I make some notes in my notebook. The bell is about to ring, and I notice we're the last group to finish and clean up.

"Yep. And probably more," she says as she gathers up the test tubes to take them to the sink in the back of the room. "I stay away from her. I suggest you do the same. You'll live longer." She winks at me and heads to the sink. I grab the beaker and the rest of the equipment and follow her.

"If she's done all those bad things, why hasn't someone tried to stop her?" I ask.

Chastity deposits the test tubes in the sink. "What makes you think they haven't tried?" She turns to look at me, her face turning very grave. "In second grade, after Maisie knocked that girl from the monkey bars, her sister, Bethany, showed up to school the next day with her arm in a cast. The rumor was that Bethany saw Maisie push the girl off the monkey bars and threatened to tell their parents, so Maisie broke her arm. Can you believe that? She broke her own sister's arm!"

We walk back to our table and Chastity gathers her notebook and pencil. "And when that boy fell off his skateboard, his best friend…." She looks over her left shoulder and points to the boy sitting at the table in the far back corner. "Lamar… the shy kid in the back… See him?" I nod my head as Chastity continues, "Well, he confronted Maisie after school, but he was stupid and did it with no witnesses around. He accused her of hurting his friend on purpose and blamed her for the kid's broken leg. She punched him and broke his nose. They ended up in the principal's office, but it was his word against hers. She said he tried to beat her up, tried to jump her behind the school, and she was defending herself. But that's a load of bull. I mean, look at him!" As I glance at Lamar, the bell rings. He picks up his books and walks past me out of the room. He's several inches shorter than me and skinny as a rail. There's no way he could beat up Maisie. He's lucky she only broke his nose.

Chastity swings her bag over her shoulder. "You'll learn that everyone here falls into one of two groups: those who are friends with Maisie because they think they're safer that way, and those who stay as far away from her as possible. I'm in the second group. I suggest you join me." She gives me a half-smile and walks out of class.

My head's swimming. I collect my books and head to my last class. I'm half the way to my classroom before I realize I'm supposed to go to the band room instead, and I have to turn around and double-time it there so I'm not late. I scan the halls for signs of Maisie, but she is conspicuously absent.

Band class is rather comical. Not only does Mr. Murphy need a piccolo player, but he needs just about every other instrument as well. I, however, can only play one at a time, and he already seems happy with my progress on the piccolo. I've been playing it for all of one day, and I'm already better than some of the kids who have probably been playing their instruments for years. I don't think that it's because I'm some sort of musical genius. It's probably simple mathematics. I practice a lot of hours, and it doesn't sound like many of these kids put in enough practice time. Maybe they'll get better as the year goes on. I certainly hope so.

I walk home at the end of the day, constantly looking over my shoulder. Maisie is nowhere in sight. I think I liked it better when I could see her and knew where she was.

* * *

That night, I sit in front of the blackboard wall replaying the conversation with Chastity in my head. I feel fairly certain now that the warning from Caroline Dent was regarding Maisie, not Anastasia. I decide to ask Anastasia for confirmation of some of the things Chastity said. This way, I'll know for sure. I write the following questions on the blackboard:

Do you mean Maryanne and Caroline Dent (the ones who used to live in this house)?

Did Maisie cut the brake cables on their bikes?

Did she cause the 6th grade boy to fall off his skateboard?

Did she cause the 2nd grade girl to fall off the monkey bars?

Will she try to harm me?

What will she do?

I sleep with the light on again tonight, but not because I'm afraid of Anastasia. A ghost in my house may be the least of my problems.

TUESDAY, SEPTEMBER 13TH

I wake the next morning and open the door to my bedroom. I'm still in my pajamas. Dressing for school can wait. I put my hand on the doorknob to the blue room and am just about to open it.

"Good morning, Lulu," says Dad. He's coming out of his bedroom, suit jacket in hand. "How did you sleep?"

I spin around and flash what I'm sure is a terribly guilty-looking smile. "Fine, Dad. I slept well. You?"

He laughs, "Yes, I slept well, too. Thank you. You better get dressed. Don't want to be late for school."

"Right!" I say, a little too enthusiastically. "I'll be right down." I start back towards my room as he heads downstairs. Once he's at the bottom and rounds the corner towards the kitchen, I tip toe back to the blue room and sneak inside. I stand in front of the blackboard and read Anastasia's answers to my questions:

1. **Did you mean Maryanne and Caroline Dent (the ones who used to live in this house)?** Yes.

2. Did Maisie cut the brake cables on their bikes? Yes.
3. Did she cause the 6th grade boy to fall off his skateboard? Yes.
4. Did she cause the 2nd grade girl to fall off the monkey bars? Yes.
5. Will she try to harm me? Yes.
6. What will she do? I don't know yet. But I will try to warn you if I can.

Anastasia didn't stop there. She wrote one more line below all my questions: Tallulah, all these children lived in this house. Be careful!

I sink to my knees, shaking and out of breath. Now, I'm really scared. All of the warnings have been about Maisie, not Anastasia. It's Maisie who poses the threat. And, judging by Anastasia's warning this morning, it is a very real and dangerous threat. I run back to my room and grab my notebook, which I've hidden in the bottom drawer of my desk under a pile of junk. I sit in front of the blackboard, copy down the Q&As from last night, and then erase the board. Before I leave, though, I pick up the nub of chalk and write in tiny letters at the bottom of the wall: **Thank you!** It seems like the right thing to say at a time like this. It's not Anastasia who is trying to hurt me. She is trying to help me.

I get ready for school, have breakfast and kiss Mom goodbye. As I reach the sidewalk, I hear someone call my name.

"Tallulah! Wait up!"

I turn around and see Maisie running up the sidewalk with Bethany right behind her. I freeze. Now what do I do?

"Hey, how's it going?" she asks as she reaches me.

"Fine, thanks," I say. "How about you?"

"I wish it was Friday already, but what are you gonna do?" Maisie rolls her eyes and shrugs. "Let's walk to school together." She moves to one side of me, while Bethany moves to the other.

"You know, I just remembered," I say, holding up my index finger. "I forgot my English paper." It's a lie, I admit. I didn't really forget my English paper. It's safely tucked inside my backpack, but this is the only excuse I can think of under all this stress. I start to back away from them, throwing my hands up and shrugging my shoulders to try to make it more convincing. "I printed it out last night on my dad's computer and left it on his desk. I'm so forgetful sometimes. I have to go back and get it. You two go ahead. You don't want to be late."

"That's okay. We'll wait for you," says Maisie. A huge smile crosses her face.

"No!" I yell from my front lawn. "Go on ahead. I have to punch some holes in the paper and put it in a folder. It's going to take a while. I'll catch up to you." I nod and wave my arms to shoo them away. They take the hint and start out for school without me. I run back inside the house, make up some excuse for Mom and climb the stairs. From my parents' bedroom window, I can see Maisie and Bethany walk to the end of the street. They meet a boy on his bike who climbs down and walks with them. They disappear around the corner, and I let out a huge sigh of relief. "That was close," I say aloud. Fortunately Mom is still downstairs and can't hear me.

I walk to school, keeping out of sight of Maisie and Bethany. I watch them closely, but they never turn around to look for me. I reach the school and go straight to my locker. I'm swapping out some books from my backpack when I feel a tap on my shoulder. I spin around to find Maisie standing right in front of me, a little too close for comfort.

"So, you made it. Must have taken you longer than you thought to put your report together," she says smiling. "Glad you remembered it. That would have sucked to have forgotten it and not been able to turn it in. Can I see it?" She holds out her hand, palm up.

"Look, I've got to get to class. It's not a very good paper anyway. I'm hoping to squeak by with a 'C' on it." Another lie. I expect nothing less than an 'A.' I shut my locker, pick up my backpack and start walking away. "See you later," I shout as I merge into the traffic in the middle of the hallway. I walk as fast as I can to my first class and slide into my seat. I'm sweating all over. How am I going to stay away from that girl? She's haunting me more than any ghost ever could!

I eat lunch outside and take the long way through the hallways to get to my locker. I manage to avoid Maisie for the rest of the day. When school ends, I head to the library to hang out for a while. I need to make sure Maisie has time to get all the way home before I leave. I wait about 45 minutes and then make my way out of the library, waving good-bye to Mrs. Thistlewhyte as I go. I see a couple of kids in the halls, but the school is eerily quiet. The front doors are still wide open, so I walk out into the fresh air. I stand at the top of the stairs and breathe deeply.

"Hi," says someone behind me.

I spin around and find Maisie Bane leaning up against the brick wall next to the open door. I walked right past her and didn't even see her.

She smiles. "You're certainly here late. Got another English paper to write?" She saunters over to me, arms folded across her chest.

I fumble my words. "I... uh... No... I had to do some research... that's all." I shrug my shoulders and start down the steps. Maisie is right next to me. Now, there are about a dozen concrete steps in front of the school. I don't know how it happens, but I make it only 3 or 4 steps down when I suddenly feel something hit my foot. I lose my balance and fall the rest of the way.

"Tallulah!" I hear Maisie scream my name. "Oh, no. Are you all right? What happened?" I hear her run down the stairs and feel her clasp her hands on my arm. "Can you move? Let me help you up?" She sounds very concerned. Almost too concerned. I can't see her face, but I have this strange feeling that she's smiling.

"I'm fine," I say and jerk my arm free of her grasp. I'm still lying face down, staring at the sidewalk. A quick mental scan of my body tells me that both of my knees and the palms of my hands are on fire. I don't think anything is broken, since the pain isn't excruciating. I turn my hands over to see that

76

my palms are bright red. My left palm is scraped pretty badly and bleeding. My right one looks a bit better. I roll onto my side and sit up. Both my knees are bleeding. The right is much worse than the left one, and there are already lines of blood making their way down my right shin towards my sock. On my left knee, the blood is starting to bubble to the surface.

Maisie walks around me, puts her hands under my armpits and hoists me up before I can object. She's surprisingly strong for someone who's not much bigger than I am. She holds on to me until I steady myself. My right knee is throbbing and it hurts to stand on it. I take a few steps to see if I'll be able to walk, and it feels like I might be able to. I still don't look at Maisie.

"Are you going to be okay?" she asks again in a voice that drips with concern.

"Yeah, I'm fine." I reposition my backpack on my shoulders and bend down to pick up my piccolo case. When I stand up, my head swims for a moment. I breathe deeply and wait for the dizziness to pass, and then I take a few more steps away from the stairs before turning to face Maisie. She has one hand on her cheek and her eyes are wide, eyebrows raised.

"Are you sure? Maybe you should sit down? Or go back in and see the nurse?" She takes a step towards me.

"No!" I shout, holding up my bloody left hand to stop her. "I said I'm fine. I'm going home now."

"Oh, that's not a good idea." Maisie shakes her head and puts her hands on her hips. "If you can wait about 15 minutes, then I'll walk with you. Bethany has detention today, but she'll be out soon. As soon as she is, we can both walk you home. You can put your arms over our shoulders, and we'll help you walk so you don't have to put any weight on that right knee."

"Nope," I say. "I'm leaving now. I don't need your help." I turn and walk down the sidewalk. It's slow and painful, but I'm determined to get out of there before Bethany appears. I need to make it home before they can catch up with me. I hold my head up and try to walk as fast as I can given the amount of pain I'm experiencing. It's at that moment that I'm grateful Mr. Murphy didn't ask me to play the tuba. As light as the piccolo case is, it still feels heavy and cumbersome in my sore hand. I can feel the blood oozing down my right shin, but I don't look because the sight of that much blood might make me light-headed again. I keep moving. There is absolutely no way I'm stopping until I'm safe inside my house.

"Okay. If you insist. See you in school tomorrow," yells Maisie.

She watches me until I turn the corner and disappear from her view. Once out of sight, I burst into tears. I don't stop, and I don't look at my injuries. I keep hobbling and crying and looking over my shoulder. Fortunately, there's no sign of her. By the time I make it home, I'm sobbing from the pain, embarrassment and rage. I know Maisie tripped me on the stairs. I could never prove it, but I know she did it.

Mom cleans and bandages my wounds. I tell her what happened and that I think Maisie tripped me. (I don't tell her about Anastasia's warning or all the incidents that Chastity relayed to me.) I think Mom believes me, and she offers to call

Maisie's mother, but I tell her not to do it because there's no proof. She gets me set up on the sofa with my legs propped up and a pillow on my lap so I can do my homework. It's almost dinnertime when the doorbell rings. Mom answers it. I can't see who it is, but I hear Mom talking. She says something about me not being able to come to the door and, "Thank you. I'll tell her." Mom closes the door and enters the living room holding a plate of brownies.

"That was your friend, Maisie," says Mom.

"She's not my friend," I remind her.

"Well," says Mom as she comes over to sit next to me on the sofa. "She brought these for you and hopes you feel better. She said you took a nasty fall, and she's sorry she couldn't catch you in time to stop you from hurting yourself." Mom hands me the plate of brownies. "She says if you're not going to go to school tomorrow, you should give her a call. She'll collect your homework from your teachers, if you want her to."

I hand the plate of brownies back to Mom. "I don't want these. Throw them out. They're probably poisoned. And I am going to school tomorrow. I don't want her thinking that she succeeded in hurting me, and I don't want her doing anything more to "help" me." I use the air-quotes gesture to drive my point home.

Mom takes the plate of brownies. She smooths my hair and smiles. "Okay, but I'll drive you to school and pick you up at the end of the day – at least until you're able to walk without limping. Deal?"

"Deal." I smile. I really want a brownie, but I don't take one. I can't trust Maisie.

I'm allowed to eat dinner on the sofa while watching television. That's one good thing to come out of such a disastrous afternoon. Dad helps me up to my room and kisses me goodnight. I get ready for bed then hobble into the blue room. I can't kneel down, so I have to write my questions higher up on the blackboard than usual. They'll be visible if anyone comes in the room. Hopefully Mom and Dad will stay out.

I grab a new piece of chalk from the box, because I don't want to bend down to retrieve the piece that's on the floor, and I begin to write: **Did Maisie trip me on the stairs? Was it an accident? Is that the last time she'll try to hurt me?**

I don't know if Anastasia can see or travel as far as the school, but hopefully she can. I honestly don't know how it works with ghosts. Are there boundaries to what and where they can haunt? I put the chalk down and turn to go. I feel something gnawing at me in the back of my brain – it's one more question that I must ask. I pick up the chalk again and write: **What happened to all those other kids who used to live in this house?**

I'm not so sure I want the answer to that one.

WEDNESDAY, SEPTEMBER 14TH

I sleep fitfully and wake up before my alarm goes off. My whole body hurts, and it is torture to take even a few steps. I fish my notebook out from the bottom drawer of my desk and gingerly make my way to the blue room. Anastasia has provided some answers:

1. **Did Maisie trip me on the stairs?** Yes.
2. **Was it an accident?** No.
3. **Is that the last time she'll try to hurt me?** No. She didn't think it was severe enough.
4. **What happened to all those other kids who used to live in this house?** Maisie hurt them all. Some were hurt badly. Two of them died. She drowned one of them. The rest moved away before she could kill them.

I stand in front of the blackboard with tears rolling down my cheeks and my heart thumping violently in my chest. It's not over for Maisie. That trip on the stairs was just a dress rehearsal. And she actually killed two kids? Does that mean she'll try to kill me, too? I wipe my tears on my sleeve and take several deep breaths to try to calm myself. I copy down the Q&As before erasing the blackboard.

I limp back into my room to get ready for school. I pull on a long skirt that covers the bandages on my knees. I can't wear jeans, because that would hurt too much; and I won't give Maisie the satisfaction of seeing my bandaged knees, so there's no way I'm wearing shorts. The palms of my hands are sore and still red and scraped. I'll have to try to keep my palms down or my hands in my pockets so no one sees how messed up they are. I finish getting dressed and scoot down the stairs on my butt, because it hurts too much to walk down them. I'm not going to be able to do that at school, though.

I pick at my oatmeal, having lost my appetite after seeing Anastasia's responses to my questions, and I seriously contemplate telling my parents. But what would I say? I can't come out and say that there's a ghost haunting our house who says that Maisie is trying to kill me. They'll haul me off to a mental hospital before I finish explaining. So, I sit there and say nothing.

Mom drives me to school. We pass Maisie and Bethany on the way, and I slump down in the seat so they can't see me. I make Mom drop me off at the side of the school where there is less traffic. I wave to her as she pulls away and then limp into the building. I don't even go to my locker. I go straight to my first period class. I'm carrying most of my books in my backpack, so I should be able to make it until lunch before I have to swap out books. Lots of kids ask me why I'm hobbling, and I tell them that I twisted my knee. I don't think anyone saw me fall down the steps, so no one calls me out on my little fib.

* * *

I lumber into chemistry class and climb up onto my stool. Chastity raises an eyebrow and smirks.

"I told you to stay away from her," she whispers.

My eyes widen and my bottom jaw almost hits the table. "How did you know?"

"Puhhhh-lease," she says and rolls her eyes. "I knew something bad was going to happen sooner or later. You moved into that house down the street from her, didn't you? The same house that Maryanne and Caroline Dent used to live in. Am I right?"

I nod my head and manage to close my jaw.

She nods and opens her book. "Thought so. Maisie seems to target kids who live in that house. I have no idea why. Mind you, no one is safe, but the kids who have lived in that house seemed to have incurred her wrath more than anyone else." She crosses her arms in front of her. "So what happened?"

"She tripped me on the steps in the front of the school. I scraped my knees pretty badly. And my hands." I turn over my palms so she can see. The left hand is already bruising nicely, turning a pretty purplish-green.

"Oooh," she says wincing. "I bet that hurt. You're lucky it wasn't more serious."

"I don't think she's done with me," I whisper as I flip open my notebook to a clean page and write the date at the top.

"I don't know," says Chastity. She pats my hand and smiles. "She may move on to someone else and leave you alone now."

I shake my head. "No, I don't think so. I think she was testing the waters, so to speak."

"Hmmm," replies Chastity. "Then you better watch your back." And that is all that's said about that subject.

* * *

Mom picks me up after school. I notice Maisie watching me. She's standing with Bethany and some other kids at the top of the front steps, but she's facing my direction and looking right at me. I ignore her and climb into the car. I turn my head away so Maisie doesn't see me wince, as it hurts to bend my right knee.

Later that night, after Dad helps me upstairs again, I stand in front of the blackboard, ready with my next set of questions: **Why is Maisie trying to hurt and/or kill me? When will she strike again? Can I stop her?**

I hobble back to my room and pass out on top of the covers. At some point, Mom comes in my room and tucks me in under the comforter. It hurts to move, but I fall right back asleep.

THURSDAY, SEPTEMBER 15ᵀᴴ

The alarm rings, and for a moment I'm not sure where I am. But then I move my legs, and the pain makes the memories of the last couple of days come flooding back to me. My first order of business is to check the blue room. I'm greeted by the familiar shaky penmanship:

1. **Why is Maisie trying to hurt and/ or kill me?** I don't know. She has always been this way. I think she enjoys seeing people get hurt.

2. **When will she strike again?** She usually waits awhile between attacks. You should have a period of calm now. Maybe as much as a few weeks.

3. **Can I stop her?** Nothing anyone has done has worked so far.

I feel my shoulders slump as I read her last answer. Others have tried to stop her and failed – obviously. That doesn't bode well for me then. And I cringe when I reread the word "attacks." It sounds so violent as I hear it over and over again in my head. But at least there should be a short peace before war begins again. I copy down the Q&As, erase the blackboard and go back to my room.

My hands and my left knee are healing well. The wounds are starting to scab over, and the bruises are progressing nicely. My right knee is still pretty raw, and the bandages need to be changed again. Mom comes upstairs and helps me with that part, and I finish getting dressed by myself. I wear another long skirt because my knee is still too tender for jeans, and shorts are out on principle. I scoot down the stairs to breakfast.

On the drive to school, I make a resolution. I will find a way to stop Maisie. If I don't, she'll end up hurting me – or worse, killing me – and then she'll continue to go on and do it to other kids. It is entirely possible that she could grow up to be a serial killer, and I can't let that happen. What am I going to do? I have no idea. Right now, I have to limp through my day and keep avoiding Maisie Bane until I come up with a plan.

I open my locker before my first class to find a small envelope sitting on top of my books. Someone must have slid it through the vent slats. I don't have time to open it, so I put it in my bag and shuffle to my first class. Shuffling is less painful than walking, but it takes longer. I arrive at my first class with no time to spare, so I end up forgetting about the envelope. It falls to the bottom of my bag when I remove my book, and there it stays until chemistry class. When I fish my chemistry book out of my backpack, I notice the envelope. I take it out and open it.

"What's that?" says Chastity, as she heaves her backpack up onto the table.

"It's an invitation," I say.

"For crying out loud," she replies. "You look like you might puke. What kind of invitation is it?"

I swallow hard. "It's a birthday party invitation."

"Yeah. And?" Chastity spins on her stool and grabs it out of my hand. "You're kidding!" she shouts.

This causes Mr. Riddick to glance over at us. "Is there a problem, Miss Van der Hough?"

Chastity whispers through gritted teeth, "Absolutely!" Then shakes her head and calls out, "No, Mr. Riddick. No problem." She drops the invitation onto the table, acting as if it just burst into flames in her hand. "I can't believe her. She doesn't give up, does she?"

"Nope," I reply as I pick up Maisie Banes's invitation to her fifteenth birthday party this coming Saturday.

"You're not seriously thinking of going, are you?" Chastity opens her textbook and searches her backpack for a pencil.

"No. Of course not." I shove the invitation into my bag. "I'm just trying to think of a good excuse to get out of it."

Chastity cocks her head and gives me a half-smile. "Don't you think her trying to kill you is a good enough excuse?"

I half-smile back. "Yes, but I can't exactly say that when I give her my RSVP, now can I?"

Chastity keeps shaking her head at me all through class. As the bell rings, she grabs my arm. "Whatever you do, don't go to that party. I like you. You're really nice. I don't want to read about you in the Obituaries." She walks out of class. I sit on my stool and zip up my backpack. I have a splitting headache.

Between my head and my injuries, Maisie is slowly killing me with pain. Or perhaps she is trying to drive me mad.

* * *

Mom picks me up from school again. I slip gingerly into the car and hand her the invitation as I buckle my seatbelt.

Mom already knows all about the party. "Mrs. Bane came by to see me this morning. We had a nice chat over coffee. She's a very nice woman. And she says that Maisie really wants to invite you to her party. Maisie told her about your accident and said that, since you're new to the neighborhood, it would be nice to have you come so you can meet some more kids and make new friends. That doesn't sound so bad, now does it?"

"What!?!" I slam my hand on the dashboard but immediately regret it. Pain shoots through my hand and up my arm as I've managed to bash the huge bruise on my palm. "That fall was no accident, Mom. And Maisie is not trying to be nice. She's trying to...." I quit talking and bite the inside of my mouth to keep from saying any more. I can't tell Mom that Maisie's trying to kill me.

"Now, Tallulah," says Mom in her honey-don't-be-so-over-ly-dramatic voice. "I think you should go to Maisie's birthday party. She obviously wants you to come. And maybe you'll make some new friends. Besides, I already told Mrs. Bane that you'd be happy to attend."

"What!?!" I shout again, but this time I refrain from slamming my bruised hand on the dashboard.

"We'll go tomorrow after school to buy a present." Mom looks over at me and smiles. "It'll be a nice time. You'll see. And if you're not having fun, you can excuse yourself and come home. It's only a few houses down the street."

I'm fuming. I can't even see straight. I don't know who is worse – my Mom for RSVP'ing for me without asking me first, or Maisie for using my Mom against me. Right now, I'm furious with both of them.

I don't say anything for the rest of the afternoon. Mom gets nothing but grunts from me whenever she asks a question. By the time Dad gets home and we have dinner, she's pretty pissed at me. I don't really care, however. She had no right to tell Mrs. Bane that I would go to Maisie's stupid party. My life is in danger, and Mom just made it worse. Much worse.

Before I crawl into bed, I write my questions for Anastasia:

Will Maisie try to hurt me at her party? Can you come with me to the party? Can you protect me?

I lie in bed staring at the ceiling. I'm still boiling from the day's events. It takes me forever to fall asleep. As I'm drifting off, I hear the sound of chalk against the blackboard wall.

FRIDAY, SEPTEMBER 16TH

Yes, she will probably try to hurt you somehow. I'll be there watching. I don't know what I can do, but I'll try.

I wipe the sleep out of my eyes and sigh with relief as I stand in front of the blackboard. Anastasia is quickly becoming my best friend. Even if we don't have a solid defensive plan in place, at least I know I won't be going to the party alone. A ghost may not be much protection, but there will be a witness – okay, a dead one, but a witness just the same. This actually makes me smile, which I think is the first time it's happened all week. I dress for school and hop down the stairs. I apologize to Mom for my behavior yesterday and agree to go shopping for Maisie's gift after school. She drives me to school and drops me off in front.

I exit the car and find Maisie hanging out on the front steps with her sister and some other kids. Instead of sneaking off to the side entrance, I march right up to her. (Well, I don't exactly march. That hurts too much. But I do hobble very deliberately.) I climb the steps and tap Maisie on the shoulder. She is actually caught off guard. I step in close to her. It's a little too close for her comfort, actually, because she takes a step backwards. I smile.

"I'd love to come to your party on Saturday," I say with as much enthusiasm as I can muster. "I'm really looking forward to it. Happy early birthday!" I smile at everyone in the group, none of whom I know other than Bethany, and walk (or hobble) nonchalantly through the open doors and down the hall to my locker. When I get there, I collapse against it, pressing my forehead against the cool metal. I'm not sure where I got that amount of sheer nerve, but it seemed to work. I made it look like I was not afraid of her and would not be bullied. Let's hope she buys it.

I don't see Maisie for the rest of the day. Well, that's not entirely true. I did see her walk into the lunchroom, but she turned around and walked right back out again. I almost think she might be avoiding me. I'm pretty sure that's not the case. In fact, I'm about 99% sure, but there is the slight possibility that she's trying her best not to run into me. Wouldn't that be something!

* * *

Mom picks me up again today, and we go shopping for a birthday gift for Maisie. I have no idea what she likes. I'd like to get her a one-way ticket to the farthest place on the planet, but frankly I don't want to spend that much money on her. We settle for a Knicks hoodie. She's such a basketball nut, and I think

I might have seen her wear something with the Knicks logo on it. A ball cap, maybe? Anyway, it seems harmless enough.

Mom and I stop for tea and cake as a treat before heading home. She starts to tell me about her plans for the blue room. I interrupt her after she tells me that she's going to repaint the entire room a mossy-green color.

"No!" I say a little too loudly and forcefully. The fork flies out of my hand and hits the chair of the woman sitting at the table next to us. "Sorry." I wave to her, wipe the frosting off the back of her chair and pick up the now dirty fork. "Mom, please don't paint the blackboard wall. Please!"

"But Tallulah, wasn't it you who thought the blackboard wall was childish? I thought you'd be happy to get rid of it." Mom sips her tea. She hands me her fork, but I decline. I only have another two bites, and I can manage with my fingers.

I almost break down and tell her about Anastasia, but I decide to save that as a last resort. "I know, but I've grown to like it. I sometimes work out my math problems on it. And it's nice to have it to draw on. Can we keep it? You can paint the rest of the room whatever color you want. I don't care. Just please leave the blackboard wall."

"What if we paint one of the walls in your room with blackboard paint?" suggests Mom.

"No!" Again, I'm a little too loud and a little too forceful. I almost spill my tea. "I mean, it doesn't really go with the rest of my bedroom. I think it's much better in the blue room — or the green room or whatever color it's going to be." The last thing I want is Anastasia scratching out her answers in my room in the dark of night. Now, I do realize that she could be in my room at any time – right now, in fact – but the idea of actually seeing her writing with chalk is way too spooky.

"I don't really think it will go with the room once I'm done with it, sweetheart." Mom pours another cup of tea for herself.

"Please, Mom." I start begging and whining. "Can't we leave it where it is? We're not using that room anyway. If we have guests stay in there, they can use the blackboard if they want."

"I'll think about it, Tallulah. No promises, though," she replies. She raises her eyebrows at me as a warning not to assume that she has given in to me, but that's exactly what I assume.

"Oh, thank you! Really, Mom, that's all I ask. Just think about. Don't paint over the blackboard wall. At least not for a while, until we're sure we really don't need it anymore." I smile and shove a piece of cake in my mouth with my fingers. Mom shakes her head at me.

That night, I stand in front of the blackboard wall and wonder what I'll do if Mom does decide to paint over it. I guess I'll have no choice but to put up some sort of blackboard in my room. The idea gives me goose bumps.

I've come up with a plan, and I'm hoping Anastasia will go along with it. I write to Anastasia and crawl into bed, dreading the fact that tomorrow is Saturday and wishing I could stop it from arriving in the morning. I don't think I've ever felt this way about a Saturday, but then I've never had to go to Maisie Bane's birthday party.

SATURDAY, SEPTEMBER 17TH

I sleep late and finally wake to the smell of coffee brewing and bacon frying. Unfortunately, there is a knot in my stomach the size of a grapefruit, so I don't have much of an appetite. I grab my notebook, check my parents' room to make sure they are both downstairs and then sneak into the blue room to get a look at the blackboard wall.

Anastasia did not disappoint. I manage to sit on the floor, being careful not to bend my knees too much, and copy down her responses. She's on board with my plan. I only hope we can pull it off.

* * *

Two o'clock rolls around much too quickly for my taste. Mom hands me Maisie's wrapped gift and squeezes my shoulder.

"Try to have a good time, sweetheart," she says. "I'm sure you'll enjoy yourself once you're there."

"Doubt it," I say.

I tuck the gift under my arm, swing open the front door and march down the street to Maisie's house. Several other kids are making their way inside with gifts in their hands. I file in line behind them. I bet none of them are dreading this as much as me. Maisie's mom greets me at the door and shows me where to put the present. There's a table in the foyer piled high with gifts. I wait my turn to add my gift to the pile and watch the other kids follow Maisie's mom out into the backyard where the rest of the guests have gathered. Once I've dropped off my gift, I walk slowly through the foyer and into the kitchen. I notice a small bathroom past the kitchen on the way to the backyard. The door is open and the light is off. Perfect.

I look around to make sure no one is watching, and then I pull a tube of lipstick out of my pocket. I borrowed it from Mom's makeup bag. Okay, I didn't borrow it so much as I stole it. It's a really old tube that has a little bit of lipstick still left in it. And it's bright red. I haven't seen Mom wear red lipstick in forever, so she will never miss it. I sneak into the bathroom, place the lipstick on the sink right under the mirror and then head straight for the backyard. I put on my biggest smile and try to fake a spring in my step as I join everyone else outside.

"Hey, Maisie," I call out as I step onto the patio. "Happy birthday! Thanks so much for inviting me." I smile and try not to blink or look away.

"Tallulah!" cries Maisie as she greets me with a big hug, like I'm her best friend and she hasn't seen me in years. "So glad you could come." She puts her arm around me and pulls me over to the rest of the crowd. "Guys, you all know Tallulah, right? She's new to school. She moved in down the street. Into the gray house, a couple doors down." Most of the kids just stare at me. One girl actually spills her drink down her dress and quickly backs away. A couple of people nod at me.

"Help yourself to some punch, Tallulah. My parents will be serving the burgers and hotdogs soon." Maisie slaps me hard on the back, which seems to be the signal for everyone to disperse. She leaves me to join her friends.

So far it's been about as uncomfortable as I expected. I stand in line for something to drink. Bethany is pouring red punch into little paper cups without even looking up. She holds out a filled cup, and I take it from her.

"Thanks, Bethany," I say and paste my best smile on my face.

Bethany looks up and drops the ladle into the punch bowl. Punch splatters both her and me. Fortunately, I'm wearing red so it's not so noticeable. Bethany is wearing a white shirt and a light khaki skirt, so the punch splatter creates a nice sunburst affect all over her.

"Oh, no," I say, still smiling. "Your pretty outfit. I hope red punch doesn't stain."

Bethany stares at me with her mouth hanging open. "Excuse me," she whispers and runs into the house. I keep smiling, only now my smile is genuine. Obviously, no one expected me to show, so I'm probably doing something right. Either that or I'm the stupidest girl in the world. Let's hope it's the former not the latter.

I grab a napkin and blot my blouse where I can see droplets of punch. A few seconds later I hear a scream from inside the house. I spin around to face the crowd and do my best "shocked" impression. I see Mrs. Bane race into the house. Maisie is right behind her, as are most of the guests. I take a sip of punch and follow along with the crowd.

Bethany is standing outside the little bathroom, shaking and trying to spit out some words. She's not making any sense, and she keeps pointing. Finally, she grabs Maisie by the shoulders and shoves her into the bathroom. Maisie spins around, takes a look at the mirror (which no one else can see) and slams the door shut. Everyone stands there stunned.

I take another sip of punch. It's not bad punch, actually. Tastes like they used ginger ale to make it a little fizzy.

"What on earth is going on, Bethany?" asks Mrs. Bane. She tries to open the bathroom door, but Maisie has locked it from the inside.

"Nothing. Umm, it was nothing, Mom," stammers Bethany. She steps in front of the door. "I thought I saw a mouse, but it was just a tissue... yeah... a tissue that the wind blew... on the floor... in the bathroom." Bethany throws up her hands and laughs. "The light was off, and I got confused. That's all. Nothing to see here." She hugs her mother around the waist and steers her towards the backyard. "Are the burgers ready yet?"

I make sure I'm in the middle of the pack of guests as we return to the backyard and form a line at the buffet table. Maisie is gone for quite a while before emerging, red-faced and huffing. Bethany races to her, and the two of them chat animatedly while I finish with the buffet line and find an empty seat at one of the tables on the lawn. I watch as Maisie pushes Bethany aside and scans the crowd. She spots me and makes a beeline for my table. I take a big bite of my burger and brace myself.

Maisie arrives at my table, still red-faced and shooting daggers at me with her eyes. "Hey, Annie and Michael," says Maisie to the other two people sitting at the table. She practically screeches their names, but tries to regain her composure. "Would you guys do me a huge favor and grab a burger and some punch for me? I need to talk to Tallulah here for a second. Alone!" Annie leaps up from the table, knocking over her chair. Michael trips over the fallen chair, lands on his hands and knees and almost takes down Annie in the process. The two of them can't beat it out of there fast enough.

Maisie picks up Annie's chair and places it next to mine. She sits down and faces me, leaning on the table and twirling her hair so that no one can see her face. "Think that was funny, do you?"

"No, actually. Michael could have hurt himself. Annie should be more careful with her chair." I set my burger down on my plate and wipe my hands on my napkin.

"That's not what I'm talking about, and you know it!" The vein in Maisie's neck is starting to bulge and her loud whisper is bordering on a scream.

"No, I'm afraid I don't know what you're talking about," I say. I'm holding my hands in my lap to hide the fact that they are shaking. I'm desperately hoping I don't pee my pants.

Maisie leans in even closer. She's so angry she's actually starting to sweat. "I'm talking about that little stunt you pulled in the bathroom. You know how long I had to scrub to get that stuff off the mirror."

I shrug my shoulders. "What stuff? What are you talking about?"

"Are you going to sit here, in my back yard, at my birthday party, and claim that you didn't do it?" Maisie stops twirling her hair and slams her hand down on the table. A couple of kids at the other tables turn around to look at us.

I lean in and whisper. "Maisie, I don't know what you're talking about. I didn't do anything to your mirror. I've been out here the whole time talking to you and Bethany. You introduced me to your friends, remember?" I try to sound as innocent and clueless as possible.

It must be working because Maisie sits back and looks around the party at her other guests.

"Fine," she barks and stands up, once again knocking over Annie's chair. She's busy surveying the crowd when Annie and Michael cautiously approach the table with a plate of food and a cup of punch.

"Here, Maisie," says Michael, holding out the plate of food. "We got you a burger and a bit of everything else. We didn't know how hungry you were." Annie nods her head in agreement and holds out the cup of punch.

"I'm not hungry," replies Maisie as she stamps past Annie and Michael, brushing aside the plate. Annie pulls the cup back before Maisie can spill it on her and stares with her mouth open.

"I'll take the punch," I say to Annie with a smile. "If Maisie doesn't want it, that is. It's really good punch." Annie hands me the punch and, with a look of confusion, picks up her chair and goes back to eating her hotdog.

I manage to make it through the party. Don't ask me how I do it. I practically swallow my piece of cake whole so that I'm ready to flee as soon as the party starts to wind down. When the last gift is finally opened, I make my way through the crowd to where the birthday girl is sitting, surrounded by all her loot.

"Thank you for inviting me to your party, Maisie," I say as cheerfully as I can. "It was really fun. I'm afraid I have to be going. I hope you like the Knicks hoodie."

"Yeah, thanks," says Maisie. I can tell she's not sure whether she should be angry or worried. Perfect!

"See you at school on Monday," I say with a wave and make my way to the front door. I say good-bye to Mrs. Bane and thank her as well. Then I walk back home as quickly as I can without actually breaking into a sprint. I slam the front door behind me and sink to the floor, ignoring my sore knees. I'm physically exhausted. That party took every last ounce of strength and courage I had.

"Hi, sweetheart," calls Mom from the living room. "How was the party?"

"Fine," I answer from my heap on the floor. "I think it was a success." I can't wait to see if Anastasia thinks so, too.

* * *

That night, I sit on the floor in the blue room in my pajamas. Anastasia must have been able to use the lipstick I left in the bathroom. My plan had been for her to write on the mirror so that someone would find it and, preferably, announce it to everyone at the party so as to embarrass Maisie into leaving me alone. Unfortunately, only Maisie and her sister saw what Anastasia had written, but maybe that was enough. Hopefully she saw it as a warning and would heed it: Stop hurting the children of 19 Sycamore Lane.

I scratch one question on the blackboard wall. It's really the only question that needs to be answered right now: Do you think Maisie will stop bothering me now?

Before I leave to go to bed, I also write: Thank you!!!

SUNDAY, SEPTEMBER 18ᵀᴴ

I'm up early because I can't wait to see what Anastasia has written. In fact, my parents are still in bed. I tiptoe into the blue room with my notebook in hand. Anastasia's shaky handwriting greets me: She's spooked, but I don't know if it was enough to stop her. It certainly was fun!

But Anastasia had written more, and if she had been standing there I would have hugged her: I left her another note during the night on the mirror in her bedroom. I used her pink lipstick. "I know what you've done to the children of 19 Sycamore Lane."

I cover my mouth to keep from screaming for joy. I dance around the room, careful not to bump into anything, and then grab the old sock and erase the board. I write in small letters near the bottom of the wall so my parents won't see: You are brilliant! There's no way she can think it was me who wrote the second warning. You are my best friend!

I step back from the wall and feel a tear roll down my cheek. Anastasia has probably saved my life. And I don't know how to thank her. She really is my best friend. Of course, it's just my luck that she's dead.

I spend most of the day in my room practicing my music and wearing a huge smile on my face. I position my music stand so that I can play and stare out the window at Maisie's house at the same time. I watch for hours, looking for signs of Maisie. Nothing. I don't see her come out even to play basketball. Maybe Anastasia's second warning did it. Maybe she will leave me alone from now on. I wish I knew for sure, but it's not like I can go up to her and ask her if she's going to stop trying to kill me.

MONDAY, SEPTEMBER 19TH

I practically leap out of bed this morning. I'm so excited. I really think Maisie is going to leave me alone. I saw her face at the party, right after she had seen Anastasia's first note on the bathroom mirror. She was scared. She was also extremely angry, but deep down she was definitely scared. After getting Anastasia's second note, I'm sure she was terrified. I'm feeling confident that it was enough to get her to change her mind about trying to hurt me.

I throw open my bedroom door and head for the bathroom. On the way, I see the door to the blue room is open. I'm pretty sure it was closed when I went to bed last night. I step inside and look around. I can see some writing on the blackboard wall, but it's largely concealed behind a mound of boxes. There was no writing on the wall last night. I didn't leave any questions for Anastasia.

I make my way across the room, pushing aside boxes as I go. When I get to the blackboard wall, I actually stumble backwards and fall over a pile of junk that Mom has left on the floor. I go crashing to the ground, taking the junk with me. I sit there on the floor, staring at Anastasia's handwriting. It feels like I've been punched in the stomach. She wrote: She's really mad. I'm so sorry. Be careful!

Dad pokes his head in the room. "Lulu? Are you okay in here? What happened?" I leap up from the pile of junk and launch myself against the blackboard wall, spinning around so that I'm standing in front of Anastasia's note.

"I'm fine, Dad," I reply. I shrug my shoulders. "Everything's fine. Why do you ask?"

"I ask because you're making quite a racket in here. Why is all that stuff all over the floor?" He crosses his arms and leans against the doorframe.

Now, there's stuff all over the room because Mom has managed to empty most of the boxes but not actually put anything away. I point to the pile of junk that I knocked over. "Oh, you mean that?" I answer, waving my hand as if the mess is unimportant. "I was looking for something, but couldn't find it. I'll straighten it up."

"What are you looking for? I'll help you," offers Dad as he steps in the room. He surveys the mess, hands on his hips and lips pursed in frustration.

"No, no, that's okay. I decided I don't need it anyway." I lean against the blackboard wall and rub my back against it, swaying back and forth trying to erase Anastasia's note. "You don't want to be late for work." I take a quick glance over my shoulder. Most of the writing is gone. I cross the room in two strides, grabbing Dad by the arm and spinning him around towards the door. "I hope you have a good day at work, Daddy." 'Daddy' always works on him. He gives me his oh-isn't-she-sweet smile and kisses me on the top of my head.

"Alright, Lulu," he says as he heads for the stairs. "Hurry up. You don't want to be late for school. Have a great day, kitten." Dad descends the stairs and heads for the kitchen.

I step back into the blue room to make sure Anastasia's note is really gone, then head back to my room. I jot down Anastasia's latest warning in my notebook and dress for school. I wait until I see Maisie and Bethany leave their house and disappear up the road before I head out the door. I make sure I keep a safe distance between us, and I enter the school through the side door to avoid Maisie and her gang who have congregated on the front steps. I do a great job of keeping away from Maisie all day, and I don't see any sign of her on the walk home.

I open the front door and feel a huge sense of relief wash over me as I step into the foyer.

"Is that you, sweetheart?" Mom calls out from the living room.

"Yeah, Mom. It's me," I answer and head to the kitchen. "I'm going to get a snack and then start my homework. Okay?"

"Tallulah, come in here, please," says Mom. I reverse my course and head back to the foyer and then into the living room. My heart leaps right up into my throat.

"Hi!" says Maisie. She's sitting on the sofa talking to my Mom and wearing the Knicks hoodie I gave her for her birthday. She hadn't been wearing it at school, and I don't know how she made it home so fast.

I drop my book bag, and it lands on my foot. Today was not the day to bring home my English anthology book. That thing weighs about ten pounds, and it landed squarely on my toes. I flinch but manage to keep from yelping. I see Maisie's mouth curl upwards in a slight smile. I can't say anything because my heart is lodged in my throat, and it's starting to impair my breathing as well.

"Tallulah, your friend Maisie stopped by to see you," says Mom. She's smiling and nodding her head encouragingly at me.

"Yeah, Tallulah. I thought you were ahead of me when school let out and that you beat me home. Your Mom was nice enough to invite me in. She makes great chocolate chip cookies." Maisie smiles sweetly at my Mom and holds up half a cookie to show me.

I think I might throw up. Maisie is in my house, sitting on my sofa, eating my cookies and sweet-talking my mother. It's my worst nightmare come true. I just stare at her. I haven't moved, and the book bag is still resting on my foot.

"Anyway," says Maisie as she lowers the cookie, pretending to look a bit disappointed that I'm not overjoyed to see her. "I was wondering if you wanted to come horseback riding with me and Bethany tomorrow afternoon. We normally have our riding lessons on Tuesdays, but our instructor is on vacation this week, so we get to ride around and have fun. I know one of the other girls who usually has a lesson on Tuesday won't be there this week either, so my Mom called to see if we could use her horse for a friend. The owners of the stables said, "Sure!" We're good friends with them. So, if you're free, Bethany and

I would love for you to come with us. It's a lot of fun, and the horse you'll be riding is perfect. I assumed you probably don't ride much. I hope that's okay. The horse is old and slow and has the nicest disposition. You'll love him. His name is Shady." She looks at me, sickly-sweet smile still plastered on her face. I can't move or speak. Maisie looks over at my Mom for help.

"Tallulah, isn't that lovely?" asks Mom. "You've always loved horses. Here's your chance to go riding with your friends."

Maisie turns her head slowly towards me and grins. That sickly-sweet smile is replaced with something much more devilish, but she's careful to make sure Mom can't see her face.

"Great!" Maisie jumps up from the sofa before I can say anything. I start shaking my head 'No,' but I can't get the word out. She grabs her book bag and walks towards me. Before I know what's happening, Maisie hugs me. With her inexplicably strong arms still around me, she says, "We'll pick you up here right after school. Wear jeans and some sort of boot or shoe with a slight heel on it. Like these." She steps back and lifts up her foot to show me her riding boots. "Got it? Well, see you tomorrow! Thanks for the cookie, Mrs. White." She waves at my Mom, flashes me her devilish grin and walks right out my front door.

"Really, Lulu," says Mom as she gets up from the sofa and grabs the plate of cookies off the coffee table. "That was very rude. You didn't even thank her for inviting you. Make sure you thank her tomorrow. What has gotten into you? I know your father and I raised you better than that."

She walks past me and heads for the kitchen without even offering me a cookie. That's fine with me, as I still can't seem to move. My head is swimming, and I'm not sure I'm breathing yet. I try closing my eyes, but that makes it feel like the ground is moving underneath me. What am I going to do? Maisie is going to kill me tomorrow! How do you kill someone on horseback? I manage to find enough strength to force my feet to take me into the kitchen, leaving my book bag right where I dropped it.

"Mom, why did you invite her into our house?" I ask. "She's evil. I've told you that. She's trying to…." I stop short of telling her Maisie's trying to kill me.

"It sounds like she's trying to be your friend," answers Mom. "And I wish you would remember your manners. Really, Lulu. That was very embarrassing for both of us."

"Embarrassing? How about terrifying?" I reply as I grab a cookie from the plate. I study it to see if I can spot any signs of tampering, but it looks pretty normal.

"Terrifying? What are you talking about?" asks Mom. She's starting to sigh a lot, which means I'm really pressing my luck. "You've always wanted to ride horses, but we've never lived some place where you could. Now you have this wonderful opportunity to ride and to make friends, and you just stand there with your mouth open, not saying a word." She gathers some papers from the kitchen table and heads for the living room. "You are going horseback riding tomorrow with Maisie, and I don't want to hear another word about it… except maybe 'thank you'!"

I'm left alone in the kitchen with an entire plate of cookies, and I actually have no appetite at all. I put my cookie back
on the plate and leave to retrieve my book bag and head for my
room. What should I do on my last night as a living person? Is
it even necessary to do my homework? And once Maisie kills
me, will I be a ghost like Anastasia?

That night I leave a note on the blackboard for Anastasia
to let her know I'm being forced to go horseback riding with
Maisie. And I beg Anastasia to come with me.

TUESDAY, SEPTEMBER 20ᵀᴴ

I'm even more depressed and scared than I was last night. Anastasia can't come with me. She doesn't know how to travel to the stables, so I'm on my own. Her only advice: Please be careful! You're in grave danger.

That's not exactly helpful.

I sit at the breakfast table with my head down, sniffling and moaning, but Mom doesn't buy it.

"You're not sick, Tallulah," she says with a hint of irritation in her voice. "You're going to school today, and you're going horseback riding with Maisie and her sister after school. End of discussion."

"Horseback riding?" asks Dad as he folds his paper and gets up from the table. He puts his dishes in the sink and comes back to kiss me on the head. "Sounds like fun, kitten. See you tonight. You can tell me all about it then."

"If I make it back alive," I mumble.

"Don't be silly," replies Mom. "I think you're going to really enjoy it."

Mom walks Dad to the front door to say goodbye. I push my soggy cereal around the bowl but give up and dump it in the sink. No sense in postponing the inevitable. I head to school, looking over my shoulder constantly. No sign of Maisie anywhere, not even on the front steps where she normally hangs out with her gang.

I can't concentrate in any of my classes. It's a wasted day. In chemistry class, I ask Chastity if she knows anything about horseback riding.

"Sure, what do you want to know?" she asks as she studies a slide under our microscope.

"How do I keep myself from being killed?" It's a perfectly legitimate question, but Chastity looks up at me as if I've got seven heads sitting on top of my shoulders.

"What are you talking about?" She steps away from the microscope so I can take a turn looking at the slide.

I swallow hard and then confess. "I'm going horseback riding with Maisie and her sister after school today."

"Are you out of your freakin' mind?" yells Chastity.

Mr. Riddick looks up from his desk. "Ladies!" he calls out. "Is there a problem?"

"No, Mr. Riddick," says Chastity. "No problem." She turns to me and whispers, "…unless you want to get yourself killed." She picks up her pencil and makes some notes in her notebook. She whispers again, "What are you thinking?"

"My Mom is making me go," I whisper as I pretend to look through the microscope. "I can't get out of it."

Chastity shakes her head and takes the microscope away from me. She bends over it, pretending to look at the slide. She continues whispering, "Make sure there are plenty of people around. You don't want to be alone with Maisie. And make sure you get an old, slow horse—one that's not easily spooked. And make sure you stay very close to the stables. Don't go wandering off, even if she tells you it's perfectly safe. You and I both know it's not safe, not by a long shot. Just…just…just try to stay away from her, but stick close to anyone else. A perfect stranger is safer than Maisie Bane." She stands up and looks at me, hands on her hips. "In fact, most hardened criminals are safer than Maisie Bane. Just be careful!"

"Right," I say as I slump over the table and put my head down on my notebook. "Easier said than done, I'm afraid."

* * *

Four o'clock arrives with seemingly lightning speed. I'm standing in the living room, staring out the window, wearing jeans and my short black boots with the low heel like I was instructed. I'm also having a slight panic attack and am finding it difficult to breathe, but that's to be expected. After all, I've got a play date with the one person on earth who is trying to kill me. I watch Maisie, her Mom and Bethany leave their house and climb into their car. They pull up in front of my house, and Maisie hops out and runs to my front door. The doorbell rings, but I'm glued to my spot in the living room.

Mom emerges from the kitchen and stands in the foyer, staring at me.

"Lulu, are you going to get the door?" she asks. "What did we talk about? You are going to go riding, and you are going to have a good time. Don't make me remind you of your manners again, or I'm going to get very angry."

I walk over to her and throw my arms around her waist. I bury my face in her cashmere sweater and hug her for a few moments. "Bye, Mom," I say. I can hear the twinge of sadness in my voice, but evidently she can't.

"All right, Lulu," she says as she pulls me off her. "You are only going to be gone a couple of hours. Now, have a good time. And don't forget to thank Maisie and Mrs. Bane." Mom opens the door and pushes me outside. She waves to Mrs. Bane, who is still in the car.

"Ready to go?" asks Maisie. She puts her arm around my shoulder and manhandles me down the steps and across the lawn. "This is going to be so much fun." Her voice is dripping with sarcasm. She opens the door to the backseat and motions for me to climb in.

I think I might have blacked out, because I honestly don't remember much about the drive to the stables. I know Maisie and Bethany spent a good bit of time arguing about which radio station to listen to, and Mrs. Bane asked me if I've ever ridden before, but that's about it. Before I know it, we're pulling into a long, winding driveway marked by a sign reading, "Tillgate Stables."

"We're here," sings Maisie. She reaches over and shakes my shoulder. I jump about six inches off the seat, even with my seatbelt on. Maisie laughs at me. "Don't worry," she says. She's once again wearing her sickly-sweet smile. "It won't hurt." She stops smiling. "Promise."

The car stops and everyone jumps out. I take my time un-fastening my seatbelt and slowly open the door. Maisie and Bethany are jogging towards the barn, and Mrs. Bane is walking over towards a paddock.

"Tallulah," calls Mrs. Bane. "Come here a minute, dear." She deposits me with Mr. Garza, who owns the stables. He asks me some questions about my riding ability and then scratches his head.

"Really, you've never ridden before?" asks Mr. Garza. "Maisie told me you were an excellent rider. If I had known you weren't that experienced, I wouldn't have picked today to have old Shady re-shoed." He scratches his head again. "I can put you on Willamena. She's the only other horse that's available. You just can't be too aggressive with her, because she looks for any excuse to run. No kicking her or squeezing your legs around her too hard, and no slapping her rump. If you sit up in the saddle and let her walk, she'll be fine."

He walks me into the barn and introduces me to Willamena. She's enormous. Actually, she's probably no big-ger than any of the other horses, but she certainly looks huge to me. Mr. Garza lets me borrow a helmet. It smells a bit sweaty, but I take it anyway. Frankly, I'd be happy to wear a full suit of armor at this point. I stay out of the way while Mr. Garza puts Willamena's saddle on her and leads her out of the barn and into the paddock. Once inside the fence, he helps me up into the saddle, and I grip the reins as tightly as I can. I resist the urge to squeeze my legs tightly around the horse's middle, because I certainly don't want her to start running. Mr. Garza walks me around the dirt ring for a while giving me some tips on what to do. I can see Maisie and Bethany riding their horses in the adjacent fenced area. Bethany waves to me, and Maisie gives me a thumbs-up, but I don't dare let go of the reins.

I'm starting to feel comfortable sitting on top of Willamena when Maisie and Bethany come trotting over to the fence on their horses.

"Mr. Garza," shouts Maisie. "Can Tallulah come with us on the trail? We promise we'll go real slow. We'll walk out a little ways and come back. What do you say? It would be a shame if she came all the way out here and only got to walk around the ring." She gives Mr. Garza her best sickly-sweet smile.

"Well," says Mr. Garza as he scratches his head again. "I guess that will be okay. She seems to be doing fine, and Willamena should be able to take care of her." He reaches up and takes hold of the bridle, escorting Willamena out of the fenced ring before I can register any objections. He turns to me and says, "Take it easy now, and don't let her get spooked. You'll be fine. I'll see you back here in a little bit." He pats Willamena on the neck. "Maisie and Bethany, you two look after your friend. Keep it to a slow walk. No faster.

Understand? We don't want Willamena thinking she can take off running."

"Yes sir, Mr. Garza," says Maisie. "We'll take it super slow." Maisie smiles at me. "Let's go, Tallulah. Just follow us. In fact, Bethany can lead the way, and I'll walk next to you and Willamena." The grapefruit-size knot returns to my stomach. It's fast becoming an old-friend. I hardly feel normal without it these days.

Bethany glances at me and turns her horse around. Maisie swings her horse wide and comes up right beside me. "Let's go," she says. She gives her horse a little kick, and it starts following Bethany's horse. Willamena takes her cue from the others and starts walking as well. We walk past the paddocks and the barn and head down a wide dirt trail that disappears into the woods. Looking around, I don't see any other riders heading in our direction.

"I don't think I'm comfortable with this," I say. "I'd like to go back to the ring. I don't think I'm ready to go on any trails."

"Nonsense," replies Maisie without even looking at me. "You're doing great. And it's not much of a trail, really. It's just a wide bridle path that loops around and ends up back on the other side of the stables. It only takes a few minutes to walk the whole thing. You'll be fine. Promise." I can't see her face, but I'm sure she's smiling her devilish smile. I grip the reins and try to talk myself out of throwing up.

We walk for a while in the woods. The trail is wide and smooth, like Maisie said. I notice it start to curve to the left, so maybe she was telling the truth and it will take us right back to the barn. Everything is going smoothly so far. We don't talk much, which is fine with me. Bethany looks over her shoulder every few minutes to make sure I'm still following, and Maisie keeps asking me how I'm doing. I do my best to look comfortable and confident, but my insides are still churning and my palms are sweating so much that I'm afraid the reins will be soaked through.

I see Maisie's horse is slowing down a bit, and Willamena slows to match her pace. Bethany doesn't seem to notice and keeps riding on ahead, disappearing around the bend.

"Hey, there's a little brook up ahead," announces Maisie. "My horse could use a drink. It won't take but a minute. Willamena is probably thirsty, too."

"No, I don't think she is. I'm going to stick to the path and follow Bethany," I plead, but Willamena isn't responding to anything I do. She follows Maisie's horse off the path and down a little hill towards the brook. The water is about a foot deep, and it gurgles softly as it winds its way into the forest. The canopy of bright green leaves is filled with birds, all singing different tunes. Unfortunately, my heart is pounding so loudly that it is drowning everything else out. Maisie's horse reaches the brook and lowers her head to drink. Willamena catches up to her and puts her front hooves into the water.

"Ease up on the reins so she can drink. Like this," says Maisie. She shows me the slack in her reins. I open my hands and let the reins fall slack. Willamena lowers her head and begins to drink. Nothing happens. Maisie strokes her horse's neck and waits. I do the same to Willamena. When Maisie's horse is finished, she turns her horse around.

"See," she says. "Nothing to it. You're a natural." Willamena picks up her head and shakes it. "Okay, let's get going." Maisie gently kicks her horse, and the horse takes a couple of steps.

I'm beginning to pull the reins back in so I can try to swing Willamena around when I hear what sounds like a slap. I feel Willamena lurch underneath me. I grasp for the reins but end up with a fist full of Willamena's mane – and I hold on for dear life. Willamena starts running. She bounds across the brook and up the opposite bank, but there's no bridle path on this side. Willamena is weaving in and out of the trees trying to pick up speed. I crouch down to avoid getting hit by tree branches. I wrap my legs around her as tightly as I can until I remember that this is probably making her want to run faster. Unfortunately, I'm swaying back and forth in the saddle. If I let go with my legs, I'll fall right off. I grip her mane tightly. I don't want to hurt her, but I'm desperate. She finds a small clearing in the woods and races across it. I'm clinging to her frantically, but I don't know how to stop her. I keep shouting "Whoa," but either it's the wrong command or she's ignoring me. We're barreling for the woods on the other side of the clearing when I see there's a fallen tree directly ahead of us.

"Stop!" I scream and pull as hard as I can on Willamena's mane, but she does the opposite. I feel her surge forward and take flight. I close my eyes as we bound over the log. Willamena's front legs hit the ground, and I'm thrown forward.

My legs come out of the stirrups, and I do a forward somer-sault. I crash against Willamena's neck. The force causes me to lose my grip on her mane, and I slam against the ground. I keep my eyes closed, bracing for Willamena to trample me, but I hear her running off. A moment later, there's nothing but silence. That's when the pain hits. All at once, the pain surges through my body—my whole body.

That's the last thing I remember until the paramedics ar-rive. I open my eyes to find a man and a woman leaning over me, asking me questions and trying to get me to move my fin-gers and toes. It takes a long time to get me out of the woods. They have to strap me onto a long board and then carry me back through the clearing and across the brook. Once on the bridle path, they put me on a stretcher and hoist me into the ambulance. I try not to look around, and I don't say much. I'm just happy to still be alive and surrounded by people who aren't Maisie Bane. I can tell Mr. Garza is very upset, but I don't care, quite frankly. I don't see Maisie, thankfully, but I do catch a glimpse of Bethany. She's biting her nails, and all the color has drained from her face. Again, I really don't care. I'm in pain all over, and I want to be taken out of here. Fortunately, it's going to happen in an ambulance and not in a hearse.

* * *

Mom meets me at the hospital when I arrive in the ambu-lance and stays with me, except when I am taken for X-rays. Dad comes later. The doctor says he wants to keep me overnight in the hospital because I have a concussion. The damage isn't too bad, all in all: a broken wrist and some broken ribs. It could have been much worse, he tells me. Don't I know it! The bad news is that my arm will be in a cast for at least a month, possibly longer. That means I can't play any of my instruments, just when Mom and Mr. Murphy had just worked out a practice schedule for the church's pipe organ. I can kiss that opportunity good-bye for a while. What really stinks is that I broke my left wrist, but I'm right-handed. I won't get any reprieve on homework. At least I'm still alive to do homework, so I guess I shouldn't complain.

After the doctors and nurses leave us alone, I tell my parents what happened, as far as I remember before blacking out. "I'm sure it was Maisie who slapped my horse's rump and made her run. The horse hadn't given any hint that she wanted to run up to that point, and I didn't do anything to encourage her. I'm telling you it was Maisie. She's not my friend. She's not a nice person. Now, do you believe me?"

"I'm sorry, sweetheart." That's all Mom keeps saying. I know she feels guilty, and honestly I'm a little happy that she does. She almost got me killed by forcing me to try to be friends with Maisie. I still don't know if Mom and Dad believe me, but they promise I won't have to see Maisie anymore.

WEDNESDAY, SEPTEMBER 21ST

I'm released from the hospital early in the morning, and Mom and Dad take me home. My wrist hurts, but my ribs hurt worse. I'm taking some pain medication, but it only works for a couple of hours before the pain comes roaring back with a vengeance. Mom says I can stay home the rest of the week, and I don't have to have anyone bring me my assignments. Flowers arrive after lunch. They're from Maisie and Bethany. I tell Mom she can burn them, but Mom puts them in the dining room where I can't see them.

I spend most of the day sleeping because the medication makes me very groggy and a bit nauseated. I'm too out of it to leave any notes for Anastasia, although I'm pretty sure she's figured out what happened.

THURSDAY, SEPTEMBER 22ND

By the afternoon, I'm pretty bored. Skipping school is fun, but I'm getting tired of lying around watching television. When I'm at school, I'd usually give anything to stay home sick for a day or two. Now that I can, I kind of wish I could be doing something else. Okay, maybe I don't really want to go back to school, but I'm tired of lying here. It doesn't help that my ribs are killing me. It hurts to breath, to laugh, to sit, to stand, to walk and to lie down. It hurts all the time.

Dad brings home pizza. I hadn't realized that pizza was a two-handed food until I tried eating it with only one hand. When I try to use my left hand, the grease drips onto my fingers. I have to drop my slice and race to wipe my fingers before the grease trickles under the cast. Needless to say, I end up eating less than my normal share. There is good news, though. Cookies are still a one-handed food, and Mom really does make the best chocolate chip cookies.

"Lulu, we're thinking of talking to a lawyer about what happened at the stables," says Dad, wiping pizza grease off his chin. "If we decide to sue Tillgate Stables, you'll probably have to talk to some lawyers and answer their questions. We want to make sure you are aware...."

"Why?" I ask, my mouth full of food. "Why would you sue the stables? It wasn't Mr. Garza's fault. I mean, he was stupid to let me ride off on Willamena without more lessons, but it was Maisie who caused her to run. She's really the one who was responsible. We should sue her!"

"Sweetheart," says Mom. She pats my good wrist. "I don't think we can sue Maisie. First of all, no one saw her do anything wrong. You said yourself that you didn't see her slap your horse."

"Yes, but she set the whole thing up so that I would get hurt... or worse!" I can feel my face getting red, and I'm on the verge of shouting or crying. I'm not sure which.

"Alright, honey. Calm down," says Mom.

"Seriously, Mom. It wasn't Mr. Garza's fault. It was Maisie's," I plead. "I'm telling you it was all her. She's the reason I got hurt."

"Lulu, we can't sue Maisie. There's no basis for a lawsuit," says Dad.

"Then just drop it!" I push my plate away from me. I've lost my appetite, even for chocolate chip cookies. Mom pats my wrist, and Dad sighs and shakes his head. We don't speak of lawsuits or lawyers again.

Before heading to bed, I sneak into the blue room and leave Anastasia a note. I can't bend down or sit on the floor, because it hurts too much and I might not be able to get back up. I have to write my note high on the wall, high enough that my parents will see it if they happen to come into the room. I move a floor lamp in front of the writing, but it doesn't provide much cover. I turn off the light, close the door and hope no one enters until I do tomorrow morning.

FRIDAY, SEPTEMBER 23ᴿᴰ

I'm in luck. Dad leaves earlier than usual for a meeting, and Mom has several lessons this morning, so she's a bit distracted. It doesn't look like either of them visited the blue room. But Anastasia paid a visit. Her shaky handwriting is visible as soon as I open the door.

1. **Do you know that Maisie caused me to fall off a horse and get hurt?** Yes. You are very lucky it wasn't worse.

2. **Will she stop now?** I don't know. She will probably leave you alone for a while - but I've never actually seen her stop until a child moves... or gets killed.

I feel my chest getting tight and my heart banging hard against my bruised ribs. I want to cry, but that would hurt too much. I wipe the blackboard clean and head back to bed.

* * *

Stacey Horan

Mom's last lesson ends around lunchtime. She knocks on my door and wakes me up. "Honey, come down to the living room. I have something to show you."

It takes a few minutes for me crawl out of bed and make my way downstairs.

"I'm in here, sweetheart," calls Mom. "I have a surprise for you."

I join her in the living room, rubbing my eyes and trying to clear the fogginess from my head. I pick the tall wingback chair opposite Mom, because it is the easiest one to sit in with all my aches and pains.

"How were your lessons?" I ask. I slept through them, so they couldn't have been too bad.

"Oh fine, honey. But, guess what?" says Mom. She's grinning from ear to ear. "Your Dad and I know you've been having a hard time lately."

I smirk. "Yes, I have. Does this mean we're moving?"

"No," says Mom. The smile fades and is replaced by something more akin to confusion. "Your Dad and I wanted to do something for you to help you take your mind off... things." She pauses and tries to regain the smile, but it's not quite as genuine as it was before I interrupted her. "So..." she says as she reaches down between her feet. She lifts up a large picnic basket and puts it on the coffee table. "Mrs. Fitzsimmons brought this for you when she came for her lesson today. Go head, darling. Open it." She seems to have regained the genuine smile now.

I gingerly stand up from the chair and lean over the coffee table. Mom pushes the basket closer to me so I don't have to lean too far. With my good hand, I lift off the lid.

"Ooooooohhhhhh," I squeal. "For me?"

"Yes, sweetie," says Mom. She's smiling so hard I think she might actually start crying. "What do you think? Do you want to keep her?"

"Yes, of course! Oh, thank you, Mom! She's perfect. Absolutely perfect." Staring up at me from inside the basket is a small, white kitten with pale blue eyes and a pink nose. She's so small that I can easily lift her with my one good hand. I hold her against my chest and put my cast under her so she has something to stand on. She meows softly and looks at me, tilting her head from side to side and glancing around the room.

"What will you call her?" asks Mom as she comes over to pet the kitten.

"Anastasia," I say without any hesitation.

"Really?" says Mom. She takes a step back and looks at me. "That's quite a fancy, grown-up name for such a little thing."

"But she won't always be little," I answer. "Besides, I like that name. It... it suits her, I think." I don't tell Mom that it's the name of my best friend, because she wouldn't understand. If this kitten is even half as kind and loyal as Anastasia, my ghost friend, then it's a good name for her. The kitten rubs her face against my shirt and purrs softly. In that moment, I forget about my broken wrist and my cracked ribs. I forget about Maisie and her mission to kill me. It feels so good to hold something sweet and pure and innocent. I had started to think that there wasn't anything like that left in the world. I can feel my eyes filling with tears. I give Mom a quick kiss on the cheek and turn away from her before she can see me start to cry. "I'm going to show her my room, Mom. Thank you!" I head up the stairs before Mom can object.

I spend the afternoon in my bedroom with the kitten. She explores every inch of my room and falls asleep curled up with me on the bed. Dad puts his foot down and won't let me hold her in my lap while we eat dinner, but he agrees that she can sleep in my room with me tonight. I wake up in the middle of the night when the kitten walks across my head, and I realize that I didn't leave a message for Anastasia. I'm hesitant to walk into the blue room at night. What if I see her? I decide it's worth the risk, and I sneak out of my room. I close my eyes as I open the door to the blue room and feel along the wall for the light switch. I stand in the doorway with my eyes closed, trying to give Anastasia enough time to disappear in case she was hanging out in here. After a few moments, I open my eyes and check the room for any signs of her. There's nothing, thankfully. I leave her a short message: **I named the kitten Anastasia.**

I hope Anastasia, the ghost, will be pleased.

SATURDAY, SEPTEMBER 24TH

I'm honored. She's lovely.

I smile uncontrollably as I stare at the blackboard. I feel like I finally found a way to say thank you to my best friend for all she's done for me. I hope Anastasia, the cat, turns out to be as good a friend as Anastasia, the ghost.

MONDAY, SEPTEMBER 26TH

I spent the weekend playing with Anastasia, the cat, and forgot all about leaving any notes for Anastasia, the ghost. Now, Monday morning has rolled around, and the harsh fact that I have to return to school jolts me back to reality.

Mom drops me off at school this morning. I'm still really sore, but I've learned how to move and sit and stand so that it minimizes the pain. I've weaned myself off the painkillers. Their effectiveness didn't outweigh the side effects, like grogginess and nausea, so I'm going to try to make it through the day without them. Mom called the school and got permission for me to carry aspirin with me this week, so I'll take that if it gets to be too much. She also bought me a wheeling backpack because I can't carry anything with my sore ribs and only one good hand. It makes it really awkward to navigate through the crowded hallways and up and down the stairs, but I manage to make it to most of my classes on time. I'm a little late for chemistry class, but Mr. Riddick just nods at me and doesn't say anything.

That's how everyone has been acting towards me. They just nod. Sometimes they look at me with pity, but mostly they give me a wide berth – like I have some sort of disease and they might catch it. In a way, I do – and it's called Maisie Bane!

"You are so lucky you weren't killed," says Chastity as the class breaks up into the normal pairs to start today's experiment. Just nodding and leaving me alone is not really Chastity's style. Frankly, I'm happy to talk about it with her, since no one else seems to want to discuss it.

"Don't I know it," I whisper.

"Can I sign your cast?" she asks as she fishes in her bag for a pen. She pulls out a pink glitter pen and writes, "Too bad it wasn't the other arm," and then adds a huge winking smiley face and her name with a little heart over the "i."

"Thanks," I say. Now my cast is half covered in pink glitter ink. "Does everyone in school know?"

"Yeah, probably," answers Chastity as she flips to an empty page in her notebook. "Especially since Maisie was involved. I think everyone is amazed you survived."

"If everyone knows how dangerous she is, why doesn't anyone do anything about it? I don't understand! Why is she allowed to wander around and keep hurting people?" I try to move the microscope closer, but Chastity reaches over and moves it for me.

She sighs. "Because no one can ever catch her in the act. You of all people should know that. No one saw what happened to you with the horse. No one even saw her push you down the front steps of the school in broad daylight. What do you expect the principal or the police to do if there are no witnesses?" She grabs a slide and places it under the microscope. "I'm sorry to say it, Tallulah, but she's too clever to get caught. Try to stay away from her."

I know Chastity's right, but it doesn't make me feel any better. In fact, it makes me angry. I let Chastity do most of the work in class, and I sit back and take notes. I don't really feel like participating.

At the end of the day, I walk to my locker, fill my new wheely bag with the books I need to start catching up on my homework and make my way to the library. Mom is picking me up, but she won't be here for another hour because she has a lesson. As I enter the library, I have to maneuver my bag around Mrs. Thistlewhyte who is trying to tape a sign to the outside of the door.

"Oh, Tallulah," says Mrs. Thistlewhyte. "I heard about your accident. I hope you're feeling better. Nasty business, falling off a horse. I remember falling off my grandfather's horse when I was a little girl. Broke my arm in two places. Haven't been back on a horse since that day." She smiles at me with a look of sympathy and pity.

"I'm feeling better, thanks. And I don't think I'll be riding a horse any time real soon, either," I reply. I notice the sign that she has taped to the door. It's crooked, but I don't point that out. "The library is closed on Thursday?" I ask.

"Yes, we have a staff meeting, so it will be closed in the afternoon. Hope you feel better, dear." Mrs. Thistlewhyte gathers her tape and heads to the check-out desk. I'm grateful that the library is open today. I feel safe in here, and I chose a seat as close to the check-out desk as I can so everyone can see me – and there is no way Maisie can sneak up on me.

I sit and study for a while, but I'm having trouble concentrating. I put my head down on my book and start to close my eyes. Someone turns the overhead lights off, and I jolt upright in my seat. In that split second, all I can think is that Maisie is coming to get me. I grab my pencil, lead point at the ready. It's the only weapon within my reach, so it will have to do. After a few seconds, the lights come back on. There's no sign of Maisie.

"Is someone playing with the lights?" calls Mrs. Thistlewhyte as she emerges from her office behind the check-out desk. "Whoever is doing that needs to stop it right now." She stands with her hands on her hips, surveying the room. The lights flicker a few more times. Several of the kids start giggling. "Hmmm… There must be a power surge or something," huffs Mrs. Thistlewhyte. She waits for the lights to turn off again, but they remain on. As soon as she returns to her office behind the check-out desk, however, the theft alarm by the library door starting wailing. I practically jump out of my seat. Mrs. Thistlewhyte rushes from her office. "Who set off the alarm?" she calls. "Did anyone see someone set off the alarm?"

A number of the kids shake their heads or answer, "No." Mrs. Thistlewhyte looks over at me for confirmation. I shake my head and shrug my shoulders. She sighs and shuts off the alarm. I release my death grip on my pencil and try to relax, only to realize that my whole body aches. The aspirin I took in the morning has long since worn off, and I'm due for some more. I pull the little plastic bottle out of my bag and walk out into the hall to find a water fountain. The closest one is outside the cafeteria, down the hall and around the corner.

I pull off the top and pour two tablets into my hand. I've gotten pretty good at swallowing both at the same time, but I've never tried to do it while drinking from a water fountain. It takes a couple of mouthfuls of water before they finally go down. I stand up and wipe my mouth on my sleeve. The fountain is built into an alcove in the wall so it doesn't stick out in the hallway. Above the fountain is a metal backsplash, about two feet high. There's condensation on the backsplash because the water is so cold coming out of the fountain. I watch a water droplet roll down the backsplash. Suddenly, I feel a chill, and then I see something. I suck in my breath, which causes a sharp pain to shoot through my cracked ribs. In the condensation, I watch letters start to form in the all-too-familiar shaky handwriting: R...O...O..F.

I can't breath. I also can't move. I stand there, as if my feet are stuck in eight inches of cement. I stare at the letters written in the moisture on the metal backsplash. It's Anastasia. I don't know why she's here, but she is. And it's freaking me out. I'm watching her write to me, and it is scarier than I thought it would be. I have to remind myself that she's my friend and that she is not here to hurt me. She's only trying to help. Then it hits me hard. Help me with what?

Anastasia starts writing again: H...U...R...R...Y...!

I shake my head and stumble backwards, dropping the aspirin bottle. It hits the ground, popping the lid off and spilling aspirin all over the floor. I turn and race down the hallway. The stairwell to the roof is at the end of the hallway, past the cafeteria, the teachers' lounge and the janitors' closet. I don't know why I'm running, or what I'm running to or from, but Anastasia wouldn't have written "HURRY!" if it wasn't an emergency. I'm in danger, clearly. I just don't know why I have to go to the roof.

I shove open the heavy door and start running up the stairs. It's three flights in total, but I can only run up one before my ribs feel like they are about to split wide open and I'm having trouble catching my breath. I walk up the rest of the stairs as fast as I can, clutching the railing with my one good hand and trying desperately to ignore the searing pain in my side. I make it to the top and find the door to the roof. Someone has propped it open with a crushed soda can. My heart is pounding loudly in my ears. I push the door open slowly, hoping that there is no one waiting for me on the other side. I open it about a foot and try to peak out. I don't see anything but the gravel rooftop, air conditioning units and metal ductwork. There is a parapet wall around the rooftop's edge that is about four feet in height. I push the door open the rest of the way and step outside. I close it carefully behind me, making sure the soda can keeps it propped open. I don't see anyone. I walk cautiously to the middle of the rooftop. I can hear the fans whirring in the air conditioning units. Their sound is starting to drown out my pounding heart. My breathing starts to slow to a more normal rhythm, and the shooting pains begin to subside a little.

And then I hear it. "Meow." It's faint. It's tiny, barely a whisper. I spin around looking at the air conditioners and the ductwork. "Meow, meow, meow." What is a cat doing up here? And it sounds like a kitten, not a full-grown cat. I follow the sounds as best as I can, but the wind keeps swirling around and the meows keep changing direction. I make my way around the edge of the wall, looking behind every tube and box and unit, but I find nothing. The meowing keeps up, though. I stop for a second by the wall at the front of the school. The view from up here is amazing, and I'd love to stand around gazing at the town, but I have to find the cat. I look over the edge of the wall and see Mom's car pull up in front of the school. She gets out, and I see her wave to someone. I realize she's waving at the principal, Mrs. Gunderson, who is walking down the front walk towards her own car in the parking lot. I think about waving, but I decide it's probably not such a good idea since I'm violating about a hundred different school rules right now. I take a quick look down the front face of the building and gasp. Right below me a few feet down is an iron rod sticking about a foot or so out of the wall. It has a hook on the end, and I realize it's one of the hooks they use to hang the big banners on the front of the school. But this time, it's not a banner that's hanging from the hook. It's a small, wicker basket.

"Nooooooo!" I scream. Anastasia looks up at me with her pale blue eyes. She starts meowing louder when she sees me and tries to climb out of the basket. She's scared. Her little toes are spread wide apart as she clings to the inside of the basket. It sways in the wind. I lean over the side of the wall, but I can't reach her.

"No, Anastasia. Don't climb out. I'm coming." I try to sound soothing and calm, but my voice is shaking. My whole body is shaking. I look around, but there's nothing to use to reach the basket. I hoist myself up onto the wall, so I'm lying on my stomach with my legs dangling behind me off the ground. My ribs are screaming at me, but I don't listen. I can only hear Anastasia's cries. I try to turn a little to the left so my legs and my left arm can act as braces against the wall. That leaves my right arm free. I reach down, but I'm still a couple of inches short. I slide out farther on the ledge. The upper half of my torso is now almost completely off the ledge and suspended above the ground, which is far, far below. I reach down again, and this time my fingers grasp the basket handle. Anastasia is meowing loudly, trying to climb the sides of the basket. I slide the handle off the hook and grip it tightly. I let out a sob. I can't help it. I feel my eyes start to fill with tears.

I also feel something shove me in the ribs, my very sore and fragile ribs. I lose my breath and start sliding over the ledge. It all happens so fast, but I manage to grab the iron bar and put the basket back on it. I hold tight to the bar with my good hand. My left hand in the cast is not much help, as my fingers scratch at the back edge of the wall trying to get a grip. My wrist is killing me, and my fingers are slipping. My right leg has come lose from its hold and is now on top of the wall, but I'm holding on with all my might with my left leg. It's still on the other side of the wall, thankfully.

I look up and see Maisie standing over me. "Don't look down." She smiles her evil smile.

"Stop it!" I scream at the top of my lungs. "Help! Help! Mom! Mom-myyyyyy!" I keep screaming. I watch helplessly as Maisie reaches back and then slams her fist down onto the fingers of my left hand. "Ooowwww. Stop it!"

"Tallulah!" I hear my Mom shout from down below. "Oh my God! Tallulah!" I can't look at her. I don't want to take my eyes off Maisie. I can barely hold on now with my left hand. Between my broken wrist and my bruised fingers, I feel my grip slipping. I bite my lip and try not to breath or cry or move. I have to hold on. Just hold on. Mom's screaming has stopped. I hope that means she is on her way up the stairs. Anastasia keeps crying. She's scared but alive. I haven't dropped her… yet.

Maisie has disappeared. I'm hoping she's made a run for it. My hands are getting sweaty, and my right hand is starting to slip a little around the iron bar. I can no longer feel my left leg. I pray that it will hold on long enough for someone to rescue me. I don't want to die today. I feel like crying, but I can't spare the energy. "Please," I whisper. "Please, someone help me." It's a long way to fall, and I don't want to die today.

"Tallulah!" someone yells. It sounds like Mrs. Gunderson. "Honey, don't move. We're right here."

"Hold on, girl," says a man's voice. I feel some strong, thick arms around my waist pulling me back onto the rooftop. "Let go, dear, I've got you." It's Mr. Harris, the head custodian. I let go of the iron bar, not because he told me to, but because I have no strength left to resist his pulling me up.

"Anastasia!" I cry. I've starting sobbing. "She's in the basket. You have to save her. She's scared. Don't let her fall!"

Mr. Harris pulls me to safety and deposits me in my mother's arms. We crumble in a tangled pile on the gravel rooftop. We're both crying.

"Please!" I scream, but Mr. Harris is already bent over the side of the wall. He straightens up holding the wicker basket with Anastasia safely inside. He kneels down in front of me, cradling the basket. I reach inside with both hands and pull out my kitten. It's then that I notice the fingers on my left hand are bleeding, staining her snowy white fur a sickening orangey-red. I hold Anastasia under my chin and fall back against Mom. All I can do is cry. Everyone stares at me without saying a word.

Finally, Mrs. Gunderson clears her throat. "Why don't we all go back inside? Let's get off the roof and go down to my office."

"Yes, ma'am," says Mom. "Tallulah, honey, can you stand up?"

I nod my head. Mom stands up first. She and Mr. Harris help me to my feet. I take one step and start to fall, but Mr. Harris sweeps me up into his arms and leads the way down the stairs. He's holding me so tight that my ribs are screaming again. My wrist is throbbing, and my fingers are still bleeding. I'm too tired to do anything but lean against Mr. Harris's chest and hold Anastasia tight to me with my good hand.

Mr. Harris gently lowers me into one of the chairs in front of Mrs. Gunderson's desk. Mrs. Gunderson tries to hand me a glass of water, but I don't want to let go of Anastasia, so I just shake my head. She places the water in front of me on the desk.

"In case you want it later," says Mrs. Gunderson. She motions for Mom to sit next to me, and she moves around behind the desk. "Now, Tallulah. I know you are very shaken up, but I'd like for you to tell us what you were doing up on the roof."

I turn to Mom and feel hot tears stream down my face. It all comes out in one long sentence with no breath in between. I tell them everything – how I went to the roof and heard meowing, how I walked all around but couldn't find a cat, how I saw Mom in the parking lot, how I found Anastasia swinging in the basket, how I climbed on the ledge, and how Maisie appeared and tried to push me over the edge and kill me. The only part of the story I change is the part about the water fountain. I tell them that I saw a note on the water fountain instructing me to go to the roof – and to hurry. I don't tell them the note was written by a ghost.

Mom asks if she can speak to Mrs. Gunderson alone, so Mr. Harris escorts me out of the office and sits with me in the waiting area.

"That's a really pretty cat," says Mr. Harris. "Could I hold her for a moment? I want to check her over to make sure she's not hurt. Would that be alright?"

"What? Um... I guess," I say. It hadn't occurred to me that Anastasia might be hurt. Mr. Harris takes her from me and starts stroking her gently. He scratches her cheek and between her eyes, and pretty soon she's purring like a motorboat. He turns her over and gently squeezes her legs, looking for any sign that she's hurt. She thinks it's all a game and tries to swat him with her tiny paws.

"She looks fine to me," says Mr. Harris, handing her back to me.

"Thank you," I say.

"Oh, it's nothing," answers Mr. Harris. "I have two cats myself. Big ol' tabby cats."

"No... I mean...," I stammer. "Thank you for saving my life." I feel a tear roll down my cheek. I try to wipe it away with my hurt hand, but I end up smearing it with my cast.

"No need to thank me," he says. "I'm just glad you're safe. That was a pretty scary thing you did today. You really should have called for an adult to help you. You shouldn't have tried to rescue her on your own."

I hang my head and rub my cheek against Anastasia's soft fur. "I know, but I couldn't think straight when I found her. I panicked and just had to try to reach her. I'm sorry. I really am sorry." I bury my face against Anastasia. She thinks it's another game and starts pawing my face.

"Oh, don't cry now," says Mr. Harris.

The principal's door opens, and Mom comes out with Mrs. Gunderson.

"Tallulah, honey," says Mom soothingly as she sits next to me and strokes my hair. "Mrs. Gunderson has called the police. We're going to need you to tell them what happened. Okay, sweetie? So, we're going to stick around for a little while until they get here."

"Do we have to?" I ask. I don't know what good it will do. As Chastity said, there were no witnesses. There never are.

"Yes, sweetheart, we have to," says Mom. "Why don't I get us something to drink? Is there a vending machine around here somewhere?"

"I'll take care of it," offers Mr. Harris, and he darts from the room.

He comes back a few minutes later with two cans of soda, a candy bar and a bag of chips. Mom pops the top on a can of root beer for me.

"Why don't I hold her for a bit," says Mr. Harris. "Give you a little break and let you eat something." He takes Anastasia out of my hand before I can object. She's purring a few seconds later. How does he do that?

"Can I have the candy bar?" I ask Mom. She laughs and nods her head. I don't really have an appetite, but I feel weak. I'm hoping some sugar will help.

By the time I've finished the last bite of the candy bar, the police have arrived and Mrs. Gunderson escorts them into her office. She takes Mom and me in to see them first. Mr. Harris offers to babysit Anastasia while I talk to the police, and Mom thanks him for me. I don't really want to part with her, but Mom doesn't leave me any choice. Besides, Anastasia is curled up in the crook of his elbow sound asleep.

I tell the two policemen everything that happened, but I leave out the part about a ghost writing in the moisture on the water fountain backsplash. The police talk to everyone in turn, but I know what they are all going to say. No one saw Maisie up on the roof, so there's no proof that she tried to push me off.

Dad arrives as I'm finishing my interview with the police. He and I go for a walk down the hall to the library so I can retrieve my book bag while the police talk to Mom, Mrs. Gunderson and Mr. Harris. I carry Anastasia with me. She seems to have forgotten all about the basket and almost plummeting to her death. I wish I could forget.

Dad is exceptionally quiet after I tell him what happened, minus the part about the ghost. He puts his arm around me and kisses the top of my head. We sit together on the front steps of the school until Mom comes out and tells us we can go home. I ride home with her, and Dad follows behind.

We order pizza again (my request, not theirs) and sit around the table in the kitchen. My appetite has returned, and I manage to eat my usual share of pizza even with only one good hand.

"Sweetheart," says Mom. She's picking at her pizza and not looking at me. I can tell she's trying to choose her words carefully. "I spoke with Mrs. Gunderson, and she thinks it would be a good idea for you to talk to someone. We're worried about you. You seem to be a little… preoccupied, let's say… with Maisie… thinking she's trying to hurt you."

"But she is trying to hurt me! She tried to kill me today! She tried to kill me at the stables! She pushed me down the stairs at school!" I throw down my napkin and stand up from the table, knocking my chair over and spilling my glass of milk.

"You don't believe me, do you? You've seen what's happened to me. I didn't try to push myself off the roof. I didn't put Anastasia in a basket and hang her from the top of the school. I didn't try to kill her. I didn't try to kill myself…." I stop and stare at them both. They are looking at me with such pain in their eyes that I feel myself stop breathing. "But that's what you think, isn't it?" I take a step back, almost tripping over my chair. "You think I tried to kill myself today. That's what you think, isn't it?"

"Sweetheart, we don't know what to think," says Mom softly. "We know it's not like you to do something like that, but there was no one on the roof with you. You were all alone up there, and I can't bear to think what would have happened if we hadn't reached you in time." She covers her mouth with her hand and turns her head away from me. I can see her shoulders start to shake, so I know she's crying.

Dad turns and reaches out his hand to me. "Please, Lulu. We want to help you. We believe you. We really do. But we don't have any evidence that Maisie actually tried to hurt you today. I wish we did. Lord knows I wish we did. But we don't. And until we can find a way to do something about this, we need you to talk to someone." He leans forward and grabs my hand since I've refused to offer it to him. "Lulu, please. Mrs. Gunderson has recommended someone. A psychologist. We're going to make an appointment for you to see her. It might be helpful for you if you tell her what's been going on and how you've been feeling about everything. Will you do this? For me?" He looks so sad and scared that I nod my head.

I'm so weary from the day and from the fear I've been carrying around with me for weeks that I give in. I don't have any energy left to fight him on this. He and Mom look so pathetic that it breaks my heart.

"Fine," I say. "I'll see whoever you want. But I'm not the one who should be talking to someone. Maisie's the one who needs help. Why isn't anyone making her talk to a psychologist?"

"Mrs. Gunderson and the police will deal with Maisie," answers Dad. "I want you to stay away from her as much as possible until we can sort everything out."

"I've been trying to stay away from her! Look how well that's been going so far." I pull my hand away from his and head upstairs to my room. I'm in no mood to do my homework, so I put on my pajamas and crawl into bed with Anastasia. She curls up in my lap and falls asleep while I read a book. Mom and Dad come to say goodnight and turn in early themselves. Once I'm sure they're asleep, I sneak into the blue room.

I leave a note for Anastasia: **You saved Anastasia's life. Thank you! How did you know? How did you find me at school? Did you see Maisie try to push me off the roof? How do I stop her?**

TUESDAY, SEPTEMBER 27TH

I'm sore all over. Getting out of bed is a painful task. I am so tired of feeling sore and tired. I sneak into the blue room before getting dressed for school and heading downstairs to breakfast. Anastasia's writing greets me:

Glad you reached the kitten in time. Maisie snuck into your house and stole her while your Mom was teaching. I found you at school and tried to warn you. I made the lights flicker and set off the alarm in the library, but that didn't work. I'm glad you were thirsty! Maisie actually left the roof to go find you after hanging the kitten in the basket. I thought there was enough time for you to rescue the kitten, but Maisie saw you run to the stairs and followed you up to the roof. I couldn't stop her. I saw her push you. I'm so sorry! I didn't mean to put you in harms way, but I'm very glad you're safe. She will probably try again if we don't stop her. We need a plan. We need witnesses - other than just me.

She's right. That's what everyone has been saying. I erase the board and leave Anastasia another note: **I'll think of something.**

I have to come up with a plan. My life depends on it.

* * *

Somehow word has gotten out at school about my rooftop adventures, and there are a whole host of rumors flying around. One is that Maisie tried to push me off the roof. Another is that I tried to jump off. I like the one I overheard some kid reciting in the lunchroom. He said I was trying to board an alien spaceship, but the aliens took off before I could get on board because they saw Mrs. Gunderson in the parking lot. That one is definitely my favorite.

I walk into chemistry class and Chastity ambushes me at the door. She grabs my wheely bag and helps me over to our table.

"What is going on?" She pulls out my stool and pats the seat for me to sit down. "I've heard all kinds of rumors about you today. I'm guessing the truth involves Maisie luring you up to the roof and trying to push you off. Am I right?"

"Something like that," I say. She holds open my bag so I can pull out my textbook. "Let's just say there were no witnesses… again."

"I knew it," replies Chastity, shaking her head. She flips the pages in her book until she finds today's lesson. "I know you don't want to hear this, especially not right now, but you have to trap her. She's like a wild animal. She'll keep trying to kill you unless you trap her. You've got to get her to try something when there are people around, but preferably when she doesn't know she's being watched."

"Perfect!" I say as I roll my eyes. "And how do you suggest I do that without actually getting myself killed?"

Chastity stops what she's doing and turns to face me. She looks more serious than I've ever seen her. "I don't know, Tallulah," she says softly. "I really don't know. I'll try to think of something, some way to help you. But you have to stop her… or she will kill you." She pats my hand. "I'll help you anyway I can."

"Thanks," I say. "I don't know what I'm going to do. I agree that I have to have witnesses or no one will ever believe me, but I really don't want to get close enough for her to hurt me again."

"I know," replies Chastity. "If we could catch her on video or have a bunch of people hiding somewhere…"

I shake my head. "The problem is that she's been calling the shots. I've been caught off guard every time. I have no idea what she has planned … or when… or where."

"Maybe we can turn the tables on her," says Chastity. She grabs a couple of test tubes and starts to head to the back of the class to fill them up with today's mystery fluids, but she turns around after a couple of steps and comes back. "It's like trying to get a cobra to strike. If you provoke it enough, it will try to bite you. I know you don't want to provoke Maisie, but you have to control the situation. You have to call the shots. You have to have the element of surprise… and hope she tries to bite you." She walks off, leaving me with an image in my head of Maisie with huge fangs trying to bite me. I shudder, but I think Chastity might be on to something.

By the time Chastity returns with the liquid-filled test tubes, I'm starting to hatch a plan. "How many kids do you think you could round up after school one day?"

"I don't know," says Chastity. She shrugs as she puts the test tubes in their stand and starts reading the directions in the book. "Depends on the day. If it's Tuesday or Thursday, I can probably get the girls from the lacrosse team to help. We have practice after school on those days, but there's a 45-minute gap between the last bell and the start of practice. Why? What are you thinking?"

"That's perfect!" I've seen some of the girls on Chastity's lacrosse team. They're the kind of girls you'd want on your side in a fight, that's for sure. "I don't have the details yet, but I'm working on it. Do you think you could convince them to help me this Thursday? And ask them to bring their camera phones—because taking video will be crucial."

"You got it," smiles Chastity. "I'll talk to them at practice today. You let me know when and where by Thursday morning, and I'll have them there... with bells on!"

"No bells. We're going stealth mode." I laugh even though it hurts my ribs. It feels good to laugh. I'd almost forgotten how to do it.

* * *

After school, Mom tells me she's made an appointment for me with the psychologist for Friday afternoon right after school.

"Great!" I say. She's a bit shocked but pleased. I'm just happy it's not Thursday after school. I don't care where I have to go or who I have to talk to, but it can't happen on Thursday afternoon. I spend the rest of the afternoon and evening working on my plan, but it all hinges on one very key aspect... or, rather, one very key ghost.

I sketch out my rough plan for Anastasia on the blackboard wall before heading to bed. I hope she can help. If she can't, I'm screwed.

WEDNESDAY, SEPTEMBER 28TH

I wake up extra early because I'm so excited. I hear the shower going in my parents' bathroom, and one of them is downstairs banging around in the kitchen. I sneak into the blue room and read Anastasia's reply: Yes! I will help. I will watch Maisie today to see what I'll be able to do. You should stay away from her until Thursday.

I smile at the thought of Maisie being haunted all day. I'm so glad Anastasia is willing to help. We'll finalize the details tonight. With a ghost like Anastasia and some girls from the lacrosse team, I might be able to pull this off.

* * *

Chastity comes bouncing into chemistry class, grinning from ear to ear. "Good news," she sings. "They're in. All of them. We'll all meet right after the last bell tomorrow and do whatever you need us to do. Let me know where. And, by the way, they're never without their camera phones, so we're golden." Her giddiness is infectious, and I can't help but start to get excited.

"That's fantastic," I say. "I can't thank you and your friends enough. Can you come to school early tomorrow? I'll meet you outside your locker and give you all the details. Will you be able to spread the word to your teammates during the day? Oh, and make sure they keep it a secret. We can't risk Maisie hearing about it."

"Don't worry," replies Chastity, waving the idea away with her hand. "They won't tell a soul. None of them likes Maisie very much. A couple of them even offered to beat her up for you."

"I don't think that will be necessary, but let's keep it as a Plan B." I flip open my notebook as Mr. Riddick starts to give his lecture. I don't do a very good job of taking notes and neither does Chastity. We're too excited to concentrate.

* * *

By the time I'm ready for bed, I've worked out the details of my plan in my head. I sneak into the blue room to find that Anastasia has been hard at work herself. She has left some details of her own on the blackboard:

1st = Room 204
2nd = Room 310
3rd = Room 301
4th = Room 207
5th = Room 208
6th = Room 202
7th = Room 314
What time and where?

She's brilliant, this ghost friend of mine. She's figured out where Maisie's classes are throughout the day. That's going to be important. That's where we're going to "provoke" her, as Chastity would say. I sketch out the rest of the details for Anastasia and head to bed with a smile on my face.

I lie awake thinking about my plan. The grapefruit-size knot is back in my stomach. As much as I try, it's hard not to think about what might happen if my plan fails. I know the risk, and it's huge. But I promise myself that I'm only going to focus on the plan and doing what I need to do. And this time I have help. It's me, a whole lacrosse team and a kick-ass ghost against one psychopathic killer. That's a fairer fight, I think.

THURSDAY, SEPTEMBER 29ᵀᴴ

I set my alarm and wake up extra early because there is a lot to do today. I race to the blue room and check the blackboard wall. It's covered in writing from ceiling to floor. Anastasia is all set with the plan. I smile and close the door behind me. I copy everything she's written into my notebook, trying to memorize as I go, and I make sure I completely erase the board. This requires some careful maneuvering and standing on chairs, but I manage.

I dress as quickly as I can, given my injuries, and head down to the kitchen. I scarf down a bowl of cereal and kiss my parents good-bye, telling them that I have to be in early for a study group. Dad offers to drive me to school on his way to work, so I take him up on the offer.

I don't have to wait long before Chastity shows up at her locker.

"I hardly slept a wink last night. I'm so psyched!" she says as she comes running up to me.

"Me, too. And I shouldn't have eaten breakfast, because now I feel like I might throw up," I reply.

"Don't you dare," she says, poking me in the shoulder with her finger. "You're going to be strong today. And this is going to work!"

We go over the plan, and she runs off to track down her teammates and fill them in on the details. I head straight for the library. I wave to Mrs. Thistlewhyte as I enter and head to the back of the library. I wander through the stacks, pulling various books off the shelves and flipping through them. I need about ten minutes in here in order to make it look convincing. I disappear behind various shelves and then pop out again in the open, making sure Mrs. Thistlewhyte sees me. I do this over and over until the first bell rings. I wave good-bye as I leave. "Bye Mrs. Thistlewhyte. Have a nice day." She smiles and waves at me with a book in her hand.

I pass Chastity in the hallway. She's walking with two of her teammates, and all three of them nod at me and keep walking. So far, so good. I take the long way to class on purpose. There are only a few minutes left until the late bell rings, but I slow down when I get to the second floor. I see Maisie ahead of me in the crowd. I speed up again until I'm five feet behind her. Her teacher is standing in the hallway, as are the other teachers, so I feel safe. They always stand in the hallways before and in between classes. This is a key fact that I've counted on today.

Maisie greets her teacher and enters classroom 204. I walk close to the wall and slow down as I pass the classroom. There are large picture windows on either side the classroom door. Every classroom is constructed the same way, with large windows on either side of the doorways so you can see inside. Again, this is a fact I've counted on today.

As I pass, I see Maisie walk to her desk and sit down. But she doesn't stay seated for long. In a matter of seconds, she leaps up from her seat, races to the blackboard and begins erasing something frantically. I slow down even more as I pass the doorway. Maisie finishes erasing and glances around to see if anyone is watching. I catch her eye before I pass out of sight. I smile. She stands there frozen with her eyes wide and her mouth open. I pass the doorway and then pick up the pace to the end of the hall toward my classroom. The bell rings before I arrive, but I have a special pass from the principal's office that allows me to be late to class because my injuries don't allow me to move very fast. I was given the pass after my fall off the horse, and it was extended through this week after the rooftop incident. I haven't had to use it very much, but I will today. This is yet another fact that I've counted on in my plan.

I enter a minute or so after the bell and take my seat. I have to hang my head to hide the huge smile on my face. The plan is starting to work. Anastasia must have done a fantastic job, judging by the look on Maisie's face. It was almost as if she'd seen a ghost. In a way, she had.

The bell rings to end first period. I pack up my stuff slowly and make sure I'm one of the last people out of the classroom. I head up the back staircase and emerge on the third floor. Once again, I move slowly down the hall until I see Maisie enter room 310, and then I pick up the pace. I pass by the windows and see Maisie frantically erasing something from the blackboard. As she looks around to see if anyone is watching, I catch her eye in the window and smile. She stands there with the eraser in her hand. All of the color has drained from her face. I continue down the hallway to the end and then head back down to the second floor. I'm several minutes late to my own classroom, which earns me a serious frown from my teacher, but I really don't care. Once again, Anastasia came through for me.

I repeat the same procedure between each class. I find Maisie's classroom, wait for her to enter and then walk slowly past so she sees me as she tries desperately to erase what has been written on the blackboard. At lunch, I sit with Chastity and some of her teammates. They've secured the table right in the middle of the cafeteria, as I've requested. I see Maisie come in and sit a few tables away. She keeps her eyes on me the entire lunch period. I don't have much of an appetite, but I force myself to eat my sandwich and behave as if nothing extraordinary is happening.

Chastity and her teammates are brilliant actresses. They laugh and joke and never once turn and look in Maisie's direction. When lunch is over, I follow Maisie out of the cafeteria, and we head to the second floor. Again, I pass by her classroom in time to see her erasing something from the board. She watches me walk by and starts to head in my direction. Fortunately, my classroom is only two doors down from hers. Before Maisie can catch up to me, I strike up a conversation with my teacher who is standing right outside my classroom door. Out of the corner of my eye, I see Maisie turn in defeat and head back to her own room. I breathe a huge sigh of relief. That was a bit too close for comfort.

I gather my courage and continue to stalk her for the rest of the day. Chemistry class is completely unproductive because neither Chastity nor I can concentrate. We do our best to look like we're working, but neither one of us accomplishes anything.

As class ends, I race up to the third floor for my final "drive-by" of Maisie's classroom. I stroll past room 314 as she finishes erasing the board. I pause for a moment in the doorway, waiting for Maisie to turn around. She sees me and mouths the words, "You're dead."

I shake my head slowly and point straight at her. I mouth back the words, "No. You are!" She stares at me as I walk away. Once out of Maisie's sight, I take off down the hallway as fast as I can. I hit the stairwell and race down to the second floor to the band room. As I slide into my seat several minutes late, I feel my heart pounding against my sore ribs. So far, the plan has worked perfectly. But now, Anastasia's part is over, and it's all up to me. I maneuver my bag under my chair and realize my hands are shaking violently. I sit on my hands to hide the shaking and try to take long deep breaths. The cracked ribs really hinder my ability to breathe deeply, but I continue to inhale through the pain in a desperate attempt to calm myself down.

Band class is a blur, and the bell to end class rings all too quickly. I race out of the room and down the stairs to the library on the first floor. Mrs. Thistlewhyte is just shutting the door as I come to a screeching halt in front of her.

"Mrs. Thistlewhyte," I pant. "I left something in the library this morning. Can I please go in to get it?"

"Tallulah, now you know the library is closed this afternoon," she says frowning. "I have a staff meeting I have to attend. You'll have to come back in the morning."

"Oh, please, Mrs. Thistlewhyte. You don't understand," I whine. "It's my lucky charm. I must have dropped it in the library when I was doing my research this morning. I really need it." I lean in close and put my hand on her arm, trying to look as scared as I can. "Please! I've had such bad luck lately that I'm afraid to be without it. I know that's stupid, but I don't know what else to do. I realized it was gone during my last class. I really need to find it. I promise I won't be long, and I'll close the door behind me when I'm done. Please!" I take a quick, deep breath, which causes a sharp pain to shoot through my side. This then causes my eyes to start watering, but Mrs. Thistlewhyte thinks I'm crying.

"I don't think so, dear," she says, trying to stay strong. She's clearly torn and feeling sorry for me. I take another deep breath and blink hard, which causes tears to roll down my cheeks. That seals the deal. "Oh, all right," she says. "Now, don't cry." She glances around and then whispers to me. "Don't let anyone see you. The door is locked from the outside, so make sure you close it behind you when you leave. Now, go on and be quick about it."

Mrs. Thistlewhyte opens the door just enough to let me in and then closes it. I smile at her and mouth the words, "Thank you." She nods and hurries off down the hall. I stand by the door and wait. A minute or two later, Chastity and her team-mates appear outside the door. I open it and let them in. They rush silently past me and disappear, as instructed. I close the door so that it looks like it's closed at first glance, but the latch doesn't catch. I take my bag and head to the table in the very center of the library in the open reading area. I hop up onto the table and wait.

Only a quarter of the lights are on in the library, so there is a dim, late-night sort of feeling about the place. The tables in the open reading area are lit, but the shelves around the sides of the library are shrouded in darkness. I can't see Chastity or any of her teammates, but I know they are here – hidden, ready to help. The lights overhead flicker on and off a few times. Anastasia is here, and this gives me courage. About fifteen min-utes pass before I hear the heavy, metal library door slowly hiss open. I stare at the dark entrance, and Maisie appears from the shadows. She takes a few steps forward and stops.

"I got your messages," she says to me. She drops her back-pack on the check-out desk.

"What messages?" I ask. My voice is shockingly calm and strong. I don't know where this courage is coming from, but at that moment I realize I should have gone to the bathroom before coming here because I really have to pee.

Maisie takes a few more steps towards me. "The messages you left on the blackboards in all of my classes. What the hell are you up to?" She starts to raise her voice but checks herself. She locks her eyes on me and begins circling me by walking around the tables in a slow, hypnotic fashion.

"I didn't write anything on any blackboards. I'm not in any of your classes, so there's no way I could have written anything," I reply, pausing and twisting around on the table so that I can keep my eye on her. "However, let me take a wild guess at what these so-called messages might have been." I hop down from the table and start circling the tables in the same direction as Maisie, keeping a safe distance from her and making sure we are directly opposite each other. I slow down when she slows down. I speed up when she picks up the pace.

"First period's note was probably a name. One name: *Carly Sissinghurst*," I say. Maisie stops in her tracks, so I stop as well. "Am I right? Who is Carly Sissinghurst?"

"What's it to you?" asks Maisie. She starts circling again.

I smile and start moving again, too. "You knew her in second grade. She used to live in my house at 19 Sycamore Lane."

"So what? So I knew her," replies Maisie.

"You didn't just know her," I say. "You tried to hurt her, didn't you?"

"You're crazy. I don't know what you're talking about." Maisie speeds up a bit.

"I'm crazy?" I ask. "You pushed her off the monkey bars and caused her to hit her head. She ended up with a concussion."

"I didn't push her," Maisie blurts out. "She fell. Happens all the time. Who told you I pushed her?"

I clear my throat and smile. "What's it to you?" I ask, taunting her a little. I pick up the pace to make sure I'm keeping a safe distance between us. "Then, let's see... in your second period classroom, you probably saw another name written on the board. *Victor Ramos*. Now, how did you know Victor?"

Maisie shakes her head. "I don't know anyone named Victor Ramos."

"Sure you do, Maisie," I say. "Don't lie to me. We've been through too much together for you to lie to me. You can lie to everyone else, but don't lie to me." I stare directly at her, not blinking. I'm trying to be as confident and powerful as I can, but I'm scared that I'm going to pee my pants at any moment.

"Fine," says Maisie, which surprises me so much that I actually trip on a chair leg. "Victor used to live in your house when I was in third grade. All right? Happy?"

"What happened to Victor?" I ask. I'm praying she takes the bait.

"He moved. That's what happened."

I smile at her. "Why did he move, Maisie?"

"He had a little accident," she answers slowly. "And his parents decided to move away."

"What sort of accident?"

Maisie smiles back at me. "Why don't you tell me? You seem to know so much."

"Well, as I understand it, Victor was allergic to bees. So allergic, in fact, that he could die if he got stung. You invited him to your birthday party. Is that right? Victor asked to use the bathroom, and you showed him to the bathroom upstairs by your bedroom. Not the bathroom downstairs by the kitchen, which is very curious because that one is closer, but whatever.

You showed him to the bathroom, and he went in and closed the door. What Victor didn't know is that you had trapped three bees earlier that day and released them in your bathroom. When Victor went in, he saw the bees and panicked. He tried to get out, but you held the door closed. You wouldn't let him out. Victor started screaming, but because the party was going on downstairs, no one heard him. Victor managed to kill two of the bees, but the third one stung him. Didn't it? He went into shock and fell to the floor. When he stopped screaming, you opened the door and got rid of the bees. Your Mom found him lying on the floor, unconscious. Victor was in the hospital for a week and almost died. Is that how it happened?" Maisie and I keep circling.

"How do you know all that? Who told you? No one knew that. No one saw. What's going on? What are you trying to do?" Maisie starts to raise her voice. She stops circling and grabs the back of a chair. I see her knuckles turn white.

"I'll take that as a "Yes" then," I reply. I mimic her posture and grab the back of a chair. "Let's see… In your third period classroom, there was another name written on the board. *Danny Vipperman.* True?"

"Yes," she hisses. "How do you know about Danny?"

"Ahhh…Danny, well…" I begin slowly for dramatic effect. "Danny used to live in my house, too. 19 Sycamore Lane. Isn't that right? You knew him in fifth grade. He died, didn't he?"

"Yes," she hisses again. "He drowned, but that had nothing to do with me."

"On the contrary, Maisie, that had everything to do with you."

"He drowned," she replies, her eyes narrowing. "There were a bunch of us in the pool. People were jumping in and horsing around. There was a lot of splashing. When everyone started getting out of the pool, we saw Danny floating there. It was an accident."

"No, it wasn't," I say calmly.

"Yes, it was!" shouts Maisie. "You weren't there. You don't know. You don't have any proof."

"You're right. I wasn't there…but you were, just like you've been there for all of the other "accidents." But none of them were accidents, were they? Not Carly. Not Victor. Not Danny." I straighten up and stand as tall as I can. I can feel myself getting the upper hand.

I continue, "You held him underwater, didn't you? You held Danny's head underwater. You got everyone to play some game where there was a lot of shouting and jumping in and splashing. You made sure there were as many people as possible in the pool, and then you swam over to Danny and held his head underwater. He was thrashing about, but so was everyone else, so no one noticed. Danny was a small, weak kid. He was no match for your strength. You held him underwater until he stopped struggling and then you swam away. Isn't that right?"

"No," says Maisie weakly. She's shaking her head vigorously.

"But it is right, Maisie," I reply. "You killed him."

"No," she says again, even weaker than before.

The momentum is gathering in my favor. "Let's move on to the fourth name, the one written on the blackboard in your fourth period classroom. What was it?"

"*Terrence Green*," she answers. "That wasn't my fault."

I act stunned. "Oh, but it was your fault, Maisie." She glares at me. I smile. "Why don't you tell me what happened?"

"He had a skateboarding accident. That's all."

"Oh, there's more to it than that, Maisie, come on." I coax her gently, hoping she'll keep talking.

Maisie shakes her head and crosses her arms in front of her.

"You dared him to ride his skateboard down Crows Nest Lane, didn't you?" I see Maisie barely nod her head. I continue excitedly, "He wasn't very good on the skateboard, was he? He had only been riding it a few months, and yet you dared him to ride down the steepest hill in town. You told him that you'd run along side him for support. That he could do it. That he was a natural-born skateboarder. You taunted him in front of other kids from the neighborhood. And you ran ahead down the hill, yelling for him to do it and to hurry up. And so he did it. He got on his skateboard and started riding down the hill." Maisie is glaring at me. There's fear in her eyes, but there's something else as well, something I can't quite read.

I stand very still and keep talking. "What Terrence didn't know is that, as you ran ahead, you took a handful of gravel out of your jacket pocket. When you passed behind one of the cars parked on the side of the road, you tossed the gravel into the road. No one saw, because you were blocked from view by the parked car. It was right at the steepest part of the slope.

And you kept running and cheering Terrence on. He picked up speed quickly, didn't he? Crows Nest Lane is deceptively steep right in the middle, right where you threw the gravel. And, as you planned, Terrence hit that gravel. He flew off the skateboard and hit another parked car. He hit his head and was knocked out cold. He also broke his leg and had to have surgery. The doctors put pins in it. Isn't that right?"

"That's your version of it," she says calmly.

"No, that's not my version. I wasn't there. Remember?" I reply. "But that is what happened, isn't it?"

"So what if it is?" answers Maisie. She calmly starts circling again, so I do the same. "Terrence moved away. No one saw anything. You can't prove anything!"

I can tell Maisie is starting to unravel. "How about the next classroom? What was written on the board in your fifth period room, Maisie?"

"*Maryanne and Caroline Dent*!" shouts Maisie.

"Right. And why are they significant?" I ask, picking up the pace as Maisie starts marching around the tables.

"They used to live in your house, too, last year," she answers. "And, yes, they had a little accident." She practically spits the words at me.

"But it wasn't an "accident," and it certainly wasn't "little," now was it?" I use the air-quotes gesture to really annoy her.

"Fine, it wasn't little…but it was fun…" her voice trails off, but she keeps marching.

"It was fun? Fun to watch your friends get hurt? Fun to try to hurt them? Fun to try to kill them?"

"Maybe," she hisses. "It almost worked."

"Almost but not quite," I say. "Maryanne was hit by a car and suffered brain damage, but Caroline only had a broken arm. That must have been disappointing for you."

"Yeah, it was," she says. Her voice is changed. It's deeper, louder. It's eerie. She won't take her eyes off me. She stops for a moment and starts circling in the opposite direction. I change directions as well, stumbling over a chair leg. I catch myself and then pick up my pace to match hers.

"You threatened them, didn't you?" I ask. "If they didn't ride down Crows Nest Lane on their bikes, you would hurt their little brother. Am I right?"

"Yes," she hisses, again not sounding like herself. "They did it, too. They believed me."

"But you sabotaged it, didn't you?"

"I cut their brake cords," she answers. "Their bikes were too big for them." She rolls her eyes. "They had just gotten new bikes, but they were shaky on them. So I cut the cords when they weren't looking. It was easy. I used my dad's wire cutters from his toolbox. Just snipped them…. I cut them most of the way through so that they would break when they were squeezed really hard."

"And they lost control of their bikes. They had no brakes, so they couldn't stop," I say.

"Yeah, they couldn't stop," Maisie agrees. She's got a far-away look on her face, like she's daydreaming, even though she's staring right at me. She doesn't blink, but she keeps talking. "Caroline managed to steer her bike to the side of the road and fall off into the grass. Maryanne wasn't so smart. She kept going. She should have jumped off or done what her sister did, but she didn't. Probably too scared." Maisie chuckles a little to herself. Her pace starts to slow, but she's still got the glazed-over look in her eyes. "She kept riding her bike down the hill. She got to the intersection at Cooper Street and... Wham!" Maisie slams the table with her hand. I almost jump out of my skin. We stare at each other.

Maisie smiles at me, her hand still on the table. "She was hit by a car. She hit the windshield and went flying right over…." She straightens up, turns her hand over slowly and stares at her palm. "There was blood everywhere. Her face was mangled, and she had a huge cut on her head." She touches the top of her head and drags her finger down the side to her ear. "Brain damage. She was lucky. It should have been worse."

"Should have been?" I ask quietly, not wanting to disturb her trance-like state.

"Yes. She should have died," replied Maisie. "They all should have died. Only Danny did what he was supposed to do."

I inhale slowly to calm my nerves. "Danny did what he was supposed to do… because he died… just like *Anastasia Levinson.*"

Maisie's eyes blaze. "Yes. Just like Anastasia."

"That was the name written on the board in your sixth period class, wasn't it?" I ask. Maisie nods her head. "Who was Anastasia?" I ask.

The devilish grin returns to Maisie's face. "She was my babysitter when I was five. She used to live in your house, too."

"What happened to her?" I coax.

"She died," answers Maisie, still wearing the glazed-over look in her eyes. "Mom and Dad had to go out, so they got Anastasia to babysit." She takes a step to her left and stops. And I don't need to coax her anymore. Her story starts to pour out of her. "Bethany had the chicken pox, so she had to stay in her room. I hadn't caught the chicken pox yet, but Anastasia had already had it when she was little. That's why she could babysit." Maisie takes another step to her left and stops. I take a step to the left as well.

Maisie continues, still smiling. "I wanted to scare her. She kept doting on Bethany. I thought that if I ran away and hid, then she'd miss me and come looking for me. So I climbed out of my bedroom window and into the old magnolia tree right outside. My room is in the front corner of the house on the second floor, and I have windows on the front and side of my room. I knew, if I climbed out of the windows on the side, no one could see me from the street. I was starting to climb down the trunk of the tree when Anastasia saw me. She had come into my room to check on me. She started yelling at me and telling me to come inside, but I laughed at her." Maisie pauses and takes another step to the left. By now, she has crept around the table she slammed with her hand. I take two steps to my left in order to put another table in between us.

"Come and get me. Come and get me," sings Maisie. "Anastasia tried, but she was too big. She tried to climb through the window and out onto the branch, like I had done, but it broke off. And she fell."

"And she died?" I ask.

Maisie nods her head. "The houses on our street are really close together. Our neighbor had a fence along the side between our houses. It was one of those wrought iron fences with the spiky arrow tips on top." Maisie holds up her index finger and touches the tip of it with a finger from her other hand. "Anastasia fell right on the fence. The tips were pretty sharp and went right through her. She just hung there, not moving." Maisie stares off into space and shakes her head. "I climbed down the tree. She was right there. I could touch her. Here eyes were open, but she wasn't moving. I ran inside and turned on the television and waited for Mom and Dad to get home. Bethany had to stay in her room, so she didn't see what happened. No one saw. Mom and Dad found her when they came home. I pretended that I had fallen asleep watching television and didn't know anything." Maisie turns her gaze back to me and smiles. "She fell… right on the spikes… and she died, all because of me."

Maisie tilts her head slightly to one side. "You were supposed to die, too. But you didn't. You were supposed to be thrown from that horse and die. But you didn't." Her voice grows louder and she takes a few steps towards me. "You were supposed to fall off the roof and die. But you didn't." Maisie takes a few more steps towards me. I move further to my left, trying to keep a couple of tables between us, but she's closing the gap.

Maisie smiles, and a shiver goes down my spine. "You were stupid enough to try to save that mangy cat. I knew you had gotten it because I was watching you. I can see into your window with my telescope. It was really easy to steal it, by the way. Your mom shouldn't leave the front door unlocked when she's giving a lesson. Someone might waltz right in and take something." She smiles and continues making her way towards me. "I pushed you!" she shouts. "I pushed you, and you should have fallen. But you didn't! You held on and started shouting, and that stupid Mrs. Gunderson saw you and came running." There are now only two tables between Maisie and me.

"Were you trying to kill me?" I ask loudly and clearly.

"Yes!" she screams. "Are you deaf? You should have died, you and all the others. You should have died. Just like Danny. Just like Anastasia. You should have died!"

I move further to my left, but there's now only one table between us. I swallow hard. "So now what, Maisie? I didn't die. You tried to kill me, but you failed. So now what happens?"

Maisie stops and leans forward over the table. She smiles her evil grin and answers calmly, "I'll just have to kill you now."

Maisie is up and over the table in a flash and grabs me by the throat with both hands. She swings me around and bends me backwards against the table. She's amazingly strong. I can't scream or even breathe. I frantically try to loosen her grip, but I can't. She starts banging my head against the table. The world starts to turn gray, and I kick at her with all my might, but she simply swivels around me out of reach. I can feel myself slipping away. All I can see are her eyes, glinting with pure evil, as the gray closes in around them.

"No!" screams Maisie, as she releases her grip on my throat. I gasp for air and turn over onto my side. The color starts to return to the world, and, as my vision clears, I see Maisie writhing on the floor with five lacrosse players holding her down. Chastity and another girl are swinging my legs around and helping me down from the table.

"Are you okay?" says Chastity gently. "Tallulah? Can you hear me? Do you understand what I'm saying?"

"Yes," I croak. I can barely talk or swallow. My throat is killing me. I'm sure Maisie has done some damage, but I'm alive.

"Your eyes are not really focusing," says Chastity. She has my face in her hands and is studying my eyes. "Don't worry. Amber has gone to get help, and Denise is calling 911."

I nod my head to indicate that I understand. I try to lie back down on the table. I really want to go to sleep. My head hurts, and I feel like I may pass out.

"No, stay with me," urges Chastity. "You need to stay awake. Come on, let's walk slowly. We'll hold you up." She and the other girl put my arms around their shoulders and help me walk slowly towards the library entrance. I can hear Maisie screaming behind me. I try to look over my shoulder, but Chastity won't let me.

"Don't look, Tallulah," she says softly. "Walk away. You're safe. They're not hurting her. They're just holding her down so she can't hurt anyone. She won't hurt you or anyone else… ever!"

It's not long before the library door is flung open and several teachers come rushing in, led by Mr. Harris. He races past me and heads towards Maisie's screaming. Mrs. Gunderson stands in front of me. She takes my hand in hers and pats it.

"An ambulance has pulled up outside," she says softly. "I'll call your parents and let them know you're on your way to the hospital." She leans in towards me. "What you did was very stupid. You could have been seriously hurt… or worse!" She pauses and pats my hand again. "But you were very brave. And thanks to you and your friends, I think we can finally do something now."

I turn quickly to Chastity as Mrs. Gunderson's words start to sink in. "Did you…" I croak, but I can't speak. My voice doesn't seem to work, and there are sharp pains in my throat.

Chastity nods and practically jumps up and down. "We did! We got it all on video!" She holds up her phone and waves it in front of my face. "You were brilliant! And she confessed to everything. I got. Denise got it. Amber got it. We all got it!" The other girl who's holding me up waves her phone in my face, too. "There's no way Maisie can deny it now. No way!"

"I've seen it," says Mrs. Gunderson. "Not all of it, but enough to know that Maisie… well, let's just say there should be enough evidence now to be able to take some action…."

At that moment, the theft alarm starts wailing and interrupts Mrs. Gunderson. I can hear Mrs. Thistlewhyte yelling, "That stupid machine!" The alarm howls for a few moments before it is turned off.

I nod and smile, because I know that was Anastasia's handiwork. I can feel hot tears run down my cheeks. It's some weird mixture of feelings — happiness, remnants of fear, and relief.

It's mostly relief, I think. I feel my legs starting to give out. All of the energy seems to be draining from my body now that I'm starting to realize this ordeal is finally over. Chastity and the other girl sit me down in a chair, and I wait for the paramedics to examine me and put me on the stretcher. The police arrive as well. As I'm being hoisted up into the ambulance, I see Maisie being carried out the front entrance of the school. It takes two police officers to wrestle her down the steps and put her into the police car. The ambulance door slams shut, and I feel more tears roll down my cheeks. I finally feel safe for the first time in weeks. My body is broken, and my head is cloudy. But I didn't die. Not like Danny. Not like Anastasia.

FRIDAY, SEPTEMBER 30TH

I'm released from the hospital after being kept overnight for observation. I have another concussion and severe bruising to my larynx, which is why I'm still having trouble speaking. Swallowing hurts, but it is getting a bit easier. I'm on some pretty heavy pain medication, so I'm a bit out of it. All I want to do is get home so that I can thank Anastasia.

I don't have to go to school today. Mom is on the phone most of the morning talking to Mrs. Gunderson. The police come by the house and ask me questions. I can't really talk because of my bruised throat, so I mostly nod or shake my head to answer their questions. When they ask me who wrote the names on the blackboards, I shrug my shoulders. I shake my head when they ask if it was me. They ask me how I learned all of the details about Maisie's various attempts to harm the other kids, and I tell them the truth – sort of.

"I asked around," I croaked. "I did my research. They all had lived in this house, and I knew I was next. Someone had to stop her, and no one was listening to me. No one believed me." I start to tear up, which makes talking impossible. The police ask Mom and Dad some more questions and then leave us alone.

Mom and Dad prop me up in my bed with my books and Anastasia, the kitten. I wait until they are downstairs before I sneak into the blue room. I write Anastasia a note: **We did it! You were brilliant. I couldn't have done it without your help. I think we may have stopped Maisie for good. Thank you! Thank you! Thank you!**

I head back to bed to take a nap. It doesn't take long to fall asleep, and I wake up late in the afternoon. Before heading downstairs, I check the blackboard wall in the blue room. Anastasia has left me a note: **I'm so glad you are alive. You were very brave. I saw it all, and I'm really proud of you.**

Once again, hot tears roll down my cheeks. I erase the board and write back to her: **You were brave, too. You saved my life. You are my best friend!**

TWO MONTHS LATER

A big moving truck pulls up outside Maisie's house first thing this morning. It takes most of the day to empty their house and load everything into the truck. A few kids stop by to say good-bye to Bethany. She seems lost without her sister. Her parents pulled her out of school and have been home-schooling her with tutors since the whole incident in the library.

I haven't seen Maisie since that day when the police put her in the police car. I was told that I might have to testify at her trial, but it never came to that. Some doctors examined her, and her parents agreed to have her put in a psychiatric hospital. They struck some deal with the prosecutors and the judge. Maisie will be there for a long time. Her family is moving to be closer to her, since the hospital is a couple hundred miles away.

I was a local celebrity for a few weeks after the incident in the library. There were a number of newspaper articles and some television coverage of the "scandal," as it is being called. There was a picture of Maryanne and Caroline Dent in one of the newspapers. Caroline looked happy, but Maryanne looked small and withdrawn. The picture made my heart ache.

Chastity and I have become really good friends. I owe her and her lacrosse teammates my life. They all got their picture in the newspaper, too. Chastity was interviewed by one of the television news shows. She told the reporter about hiding in the stacks with her teammates and recording the whole episode. Some of the videos were posted online, which meant everyone everywhere saw me being strangled by Maisie. I was really embarrassed at first, but later I was more embarrassed for Maisie's sister and her parents. I feel sorry for them. They've just been shut up in their house when they haven't been driving to and from the psychiatric hospital. Their lives have been turned completely upside down, just as mine is finally starting to get back to normal.

I got the cast off my wrist last week. My left wrist is noticeably smaller than my right one, but that should correct itself in time. My ribs and throat have healed, although I do think my voice sounds a little bit different than before. Maybe that's not such a bad thing. After all, I am different than I was before. Maisie changed that. I have nightmares a lot. I wake up screaming and clutching my throat. I sometimes dream that I am being held underwater, or that I'm flying down Crows Nest Lane on my bike when a car hits me. Mom and Dad have been taking me to the psychologist so that I can talk about my nightmares, but I don't think that will fix me completely. Mom bought paint to start painting the blue room. I told her she could paint over the blackboard wall. I told her it was time.

Anastasia, my best friend, is gone. The last note she wrote was several weeks ago: Tallulah, I will always be your friend.

Now that Maisie is safely locked away, there's nothing keeping Anastasia here. I can understand her wanting to move on, but I really miss her. It was comforting to know that she was here in this house, watching over me. She was sort of my guardian angel. She was the one who gave me all of the details about Carly Sissinghurst, Victor Ramos, Danny Vipperman, Terrence Green and Maryanne and Caroline Dent. She had watched over them all. She also gave me the details about her own death. Those were the hardest to read.

Anastasia is the one who wrote the names on the blackboards in Maisie's classrooms. She also wrote the invitation on the board in Maisie's seventh period classroom: Library @ 3:30 to meet your ghosts. The part about meeting the ghosts was Anastasia's idea. It was a nice touch, and it obviously did the trick. I'm alive, thanks to Anastasia.

I miss my best friend. All I have left of her are the *Conversations* in my notebook, which I've hidden away in my room for safekeeping. Perhaps I'll see Anastasia someday – on the other side or wherever she is – when I finally do die (which hopefully won't be for a very, very long time). In a weird way, that's something to look forward to.

Life is becoming as normal as it can be, I guess. No one is stalking me or trying to kill me. No ghosts are leaving me notes on the blackboard wall in the middle of the night. It's a bit boring, actually. But, boring is good. It's very good. Maisie may haunt my dreams, but at least she can't hurt any other kids. I'm safe from her, and so is every other child who will ever live at 19 Sycamore Lane.

Stacey Horan lives in Jacksonville, Florida, with her husband, two dogs, and no ghosts …that she knows of. Inspiration for her latest book, *Sycamore Lane*, came from her own experience moving into a home with "moving day" written on a blackboard wall.

Made in the USA
Columbia, SC
16 December 2018